PIPER'S
SOMEDAY

RUTH PERKINSON

Spinsters Ink
2007

Spinsters Ink
P.O. Box 242
Midway, Florida 32343

Printed in the United States of America on acid-free paper
First Edition

Editor: Christi Cassidy
Cover designer: KIARO Creative Ltd.

ISBN-10: 1-883523-87-7
ISBN-13: 978-1-883523-87-9

For my dog, Scout,
who gave me the ten best years of my life.
Fly away, my little girl, fly away.
This is for you.

Acknowledgments

I would be remiss if I didn't give a great big kiss to both Linda Hill and Becky Arbogast for opening up my first manuscript in December of 2004, and giving my twenty-year dream a chance. You both have changed my life. Certainly, a wonderful still point.

Support has come to me from some of the most beautiful people on the planet—especially my sister and mother, who know me to the very core and make me want to always be a better person in the shadows and essence of who they are—remarkable women. My wonderful father taught me how to read and to love it. A special thank you, too, to my brother, Page Perkinson, and his lovely family.

Along my journey, too, are people like Jenny Kistler,

a gifted veterinarian and good friend. Steven Niketas and his Café Mosaic are incredible. You guys should be in Hollywood. Gina Miller, you should be in Hollywood, too.

A special thanks also goes to Heather Campbell, who is a great screenwriter, a great letter writer and a great friend. And then, there is Terri Nelson, who is truth squared. Love to Ila Skinner and all of my friends at MCC in Richmond, who understood, right away, that my first book was important. Bless all of you.

Courage to the fine youth at ROSMY who fight for a chance to be who they are each day. One day, I promise.

Thanks to Ron, Jim, Joyce, Audria, Steve and Chris who have and work at the best title company in the universe.

Christi Cassidy—you rock!

A very special acknowledgment goes to Harper Lee who mustered up the courage to write a book that, in my mind, changed the course of twentieth-century literature. I read aloud from your book to my students in Richmond, Virginia, and they heard the power of how words can change lives. Your character became my dog's namesake. Bless you, too.

Chapter 1

More often than not, I left my dog Someday tied to the red maple tree in the back of my apartment on Stoney Creek Road before I walked the eight-tenths of a mile to Carver Middle School. I know it sounds bad, but I would rather have her tied to the tree than inside where my grandfather Victor would say things like "get your sorry ass out of the way, you stinky dog," or worse, kick her on the way from his den of NASCAR iniquity to the fridge where he would forage for his eighth beer of the day. "Move, you damn dog," he'd say, shuffling by, opening the beer can to hear the whistle and steam whoosh out of the can, the *quish* sound, his religious mantra, and then he would fold the beer tab back with his thumb, sit down, re-find the lost clicker, scratch the underfold of his hairy belly, then belch. My dog was at risk with this behavior, so I tied her outside.

Someday was the dog who, as my dad would say, "found us" by the James River when him and my mom and brother Jack were still alive. Every Sunday since I could remember, we walked the same pathway to the James near my grandfather's apartment. There was a landing with a rickety pier my dad liked, and he and my brother would fish from it while my mom and I skimmed rocks against the current of the black silty water. The waves did the push-pull against our knotted, bony ankles and we would find flat rocks and she showed me how to skitter them at an angle.

Every Sunday for about a billion Sundays my brother and I pestered her and my dad about getting a puppy. "Ask your mother," my dad would say and recast his line. So we did and were relentless. She kept her answer the same. She said that we would one day get a dog when we were both ready to take care of it.

"We're ready!" we would yell in unison.

But her pat answer to me and my brother every time we badgered her would always be, "Someday, kids. Someday we will get you a dog." She would sometimes sing it, "S-O-O-O-m-m-m-d-a-a-a-a-a-a-y."

We asked for a puppy at Christmas, on our birthdays and on off holidays like Halloween and Yom Kippur, even though we weren't Jewish and didn't know what it meant anyway. Jack finally gave up, but I was determined and obsessed.

"Mr. and Mrs. Wilson have a poodle named Chico," I would say. I told them I'd take care of it if they ever went anywhere. This was evidence that I was ready. "Saving my allowance for a leash and dog food," I would say to her.

My mom would look at me and smile and say, "Someday, Piper dear." She would rub my head and go on to whatever she was doing.

By the time my tenth birthday came around, I said that someday would never come—"Never, ever, ever," I had yelled at her one time. It was the only time I sassed back at my mom: it was the only time she ever raised her hand to me.

And then one day not long after my temper tantrum, like the darkening celestial sky had opened up and manna from heaven came down, this dark, deformed-lookin' puppy who was hanging out by one of the marshy landings just limped up on three good legs to me and my brother and started following us around. Her front left paw was cleft-like and a good four inches shorter than her others, a midget paw. *Ugly, but cool.* She smelled like honeysuckle.

After a bit, my dad cast another line then looked at my mother and said flatly, "Well, I guess Someday has arrived."

We took her home and my mom said, "Well, that was that."

I told her I liked the name Someday better than That Was That. Everyone laughed and the name stuck.

• • •

Grandpa says that, except for the damn dog, they are all in heaven and to forget about it and move on. I still think they are on the way to take my brother somewhere and they can't find the right brand of cigarettes at the 7-Eleven for my dad. They are going from convenience store to convenience store looking for no-filter Camels. At each one, I imagine my brother by the candy, my father at the magazine rack and my mom waiting in the dusty Ford Ranger staring at the people on the corner. Hell, perhaps—not heaven. Sometimes, I am on the corner where the people have no faces and am waving at my mom. She doesn't see me. I wave anyway. The shadows of my family and these faceless people shade the periphery of my waking and sleeping vision like a frame outlines a pretty picture. There they are, looming like wingless angels, hovering above my left shoulder, gnomes whispering in my ear—so hard to see, though, just outside of my eyeshot when I glanced to find them floating there.

But they are all gone now and I'm stuck with lame ole' Someday.

Today, like always, I tied her to the half-leafless maple tree and walked to school where the children stared at me because of the same faded green Wal-Mart pants I had on yesterday. I didn't care. I hung out near the blacktop when we went to P.E. and then laid in the dirt in front of me. Spitting into some ant holes, I watched them emerge, scared and disoriented, running through my sticky slobber. Almost always, I forget that I've left Someday tethered to the tree. But she is there for hours with her water bowl too low and her own ants crawling on her uneaten day-old food. She doesn't seem to mind, I guess. Someday is definitely a shepherd-rabbit mix. Shepherd because her body and face look near to one; rabbit because her ears lay back on her head like one. My grandpa Victor said that if she were a smart German shepherd then her ears would stick up. Instead, she looks like a retarded one with the way her ears anneal to her head. When they perk up, Victor says she looks like the Flying Nun. I don't know what exactly that is, but I know it is not nice. Who wants to be a nun in the first place, much less flying around like a witch or something? "Someday is not retarded," I whisper under my breath at him. "You are."

In Goochland County, Virginia, where I live, children go to school past Memorial Day. We take our SOL tests before June third, nearly three weeks before school lets out, and then we watch movies till the eighteenth. So far this month, we have seen *Babe* with our English teacher—she's cool, so we don't have to do a worksheet on it. It's supposed to teach us about fables, she tells the principal when he walks in to check. In my other classes, we have seen *The Wizard of Oz* because it is supposed to help us understand tornadoes: science; and *Willy Wonka and the Chocolate Factory* because it is supposed to teach us about adding and subtracting: math. I couldn't figure this one out but then again I'm not good at math. I was in the slow class where we were still doing long division well into April before we hit fractions and everyone got the stares. The teacher repeated herself till she looked blue like the kid from the Willie Wonka movie, but it did us no good. Carly Hasselbaum, who is about the prissiest girl in school, sat neatly in her chair and stared at the teacher like she understood. Each time the teacher turned to the chalkboard to revisit how to do the same fraction, Carly reached into her purse and applied lipstick or looked in a mirror then snickered at all of us other retards like we were ugly.

Our apartment was in a long row of apartments at the edge of a creek that fed into the James River where I have a fort no one knows about. The complex itself was the grossest looking place in the whole county, not counting the double-wide trailer park four miles away. The trash bins were always too full and the tarred gravel roads were slick from fifty-year-old grease. Our neighborhood was the 'hood. Teachers and students said it was the country projects. I hated projects, especially math projects, so I ignored what they said about it.

Grandpa and me and Someday live in the small end unit. A line of pin oaks and sparsely leaved maples covered the cul-de-sac where a basketball hoop was nailed to a tree near the sewer. Every day, Someday laid in the grass while I shot until the basketball annoyingly banged itself off of the sewer and I had to run all the way into the courtyard to get it. I got it and dribbled the ball in the grass, then I laid down and stared at the sky till Someday ambled along and laid down next to me. It bugged me because she practically followed me everywhere. She licked me all the time and put her midget paw on me when she wanted me to scratch her. I did it sometimes; sometimes I didn't. We laid on the grass and if it was twilight, I counted stars. Sometimes we watched the moon and I wondered about my mom, distance and the ocean tides.

The complex also housed Crazy Clover, an old bunk of a guy, my grandpa said. Him and Clover played cards and drank beer almost all day on most days, except for when Victor took me to church. He sat in the car and drank Coke till I came out and then he pulled a Budweiser out of the cooler for the ride home. He didn't know that I hid in the church bathroom with Margie McIntosh and puffed cigarettes till we heard the priest doing his Last Supper imitation. Then there were the Wilsons, who lived at the end of the other side of our row. An old married couple who drove a rickety Plymouth, they rarely came out of the house unless it was to church or the grocery or to a neighborhood gathering.

When I got home from school after the movie fest, I untied Someday, took her inside and found my grandpa laying on the sofa watching Court TV. I washed the dishes because that's what girls do, Victor told me once. While I was occupied with soap and dirty pizza plates and empty beer cans, Someday stared up at me with her dark eyes and dark nose. Every now and again, she rolled over and moaned and I patted her on the head and said, "It's all right, girl." This seemed to satisfy her dog conscience at whatever scampery squirrel she might have been chasing in her thoughts. After the dishes, I folded the laundry, which didn't take long, then I ran outside to the court and shot the ball.

On the weekends, Someday and me went to the fort and read and watched the creek. It was through the bushes down a sharp slope fifty yards away from the basketball hoop. A creek needs watching, I decided. So, Someday and I laid around and did it.

In my mind's eye, I can't remember anything about why my mom, dad and brother went away to heaven. Someday put her head in my lap while I sat cross-legged and read my *Skateboarding* magazine. I looked up from the place where they talked about ollies and getting air, and I surveyed the glistening creek and my claim on the land. Next to the edge of my fort, I noticed there was an old red flag laying in the muck next to some crunched soda tabs. It had a big red leaf in the middle of it and was faded from the weather. Wiping the cracked mud off, I stuck it on the end of a thick stick and jammed it in the ground.

Then I pulled a Marlboro Light from a stolen pack and lit it.

Someday does not die in my story. But if I could have killed Victor with some tight fishing line wrapped around his throat, I would have done so.

Chapter 2

On the last day of school, I ran the speed of sound all the way back to the apartment, cutting through the woods and smacking branches the whole way. I'd failed my last math test on decimals. I got a fifty-six-point-seven and she rounded it up to a fifty=seven. Ironic, I thought, as it wasn't very exacta-munde. I didn't care about decimals now, so I raced away in glee that the monotony of school was over and I could spend the summer fooling around the creek and shooting basketball and hanging out with lame old Someday. I could read magazines and books and ignore Victor all I wanted, even if he told me to do something. I would ignore him. Clover, too. I didn't care how many times they told me how dumb or retarded me or Someday was. Ignore, ignore, ignore.

Even though Matt Tunstall, Luke Snodgrass and Buddy Williams were two grades ahead of me, they sometimes they let me hang out with them. I liked Buddy and Matt, but Luke was a tow-headed tear, always cussing like a sailor (my mom would have said), and every now and again he pulled my hair and then laughed when I couldn't get away from him. White trash. He was particularly tiresome and he liked to scare the bejesus out of me and everyone else, but I put up with his shenanigans because hanging out with them was better than nothing sometimes.

The last Christmas, Victor had taken me to the Goodwill where I shopped for a halfway decent skateboard. We got lucky and found an old ZoomTre that NikeSb had put out a year and a half earlier. By March, he gave me the money to replace the worn trucks and by spring I could do a forty-five, a one-eighty, a pop and an ollie and then a fakie ollie. I wore my brother's old blue and white Dekline shoes and practiced everyday at the ramp. I could even hop on low-lying pipe set up by the ramps and slide my board for ten feet without stopping.

At the top of the Stoney Creek Road, there was a sharp slope and Buddy and Luke and Matt and me had been racing a beeline to the ramp all afternoon and evening. It was a part of our last-day-of-school celebration. Then the bets started to come and the wagers were heavy: cigarettes, Skoal and Matt's dad's magazine from underneath his bed.

"Last ups!" Buddy yelled. He did a kick-flip and then rolled slyly around all four of us. He was smaller than all of us and his dark hair draped his face in curly rivulets.

"Okay, Ms. Priss." Luke flashed his black eyes and gapped teeth at me. He was rolling his board, one foot on the ground. "It's down to this. We've all gotta get home before our parents have a nigger knockdown and half a shit fit, so this is the last big race of the day."

"My name is not Ms. Priss. It's Piper Leigh Cliff. That's capital P-I-P-E-R. Capital L-E-I-G-H. Capital C-L-I-F-F. And this is my dog, Someday. Capital S—"

He grabbed the knot of my ponytail, gritted his teeth and yanked me to his knee. Someday barked at him.

"Shut up your lame-ass stinky mouth, you dumb ass dog." He kicked her bad paw. "How about if we just call you capital P-I-P for pipsqueak. Now shut the hell up. We've got a bet going here—"

I smashed his toe and pulled away. Someday barked at us both and hobbled closer to me.

"Your dog is a retard. R-E-T-A-R-D. Do you know what that spells?" He stopped his board and then mocked how she walked. He cocked his right arm up and flapped around like a chicken.

"You! It spells you." I spit on the ground and then began to feel the tears burn the inside of my eyelids.

"Luke, shut the hell up," Matt defended me and Someday. "Let's just get going!"

Luke lunged at me mockingly while holding his arm up like my dog's and I retreated back.

"What does the winner get again?" Buddy scratched Someday on the back of the head. He flipped his skateboard up and did a one-eighty before looking for the answer.

Luke hopped on his, road in a quick circle around us like a shark and then said, "Two cans of Skoal, Buddy. We already went over this. First one to the bottom of the cul-de-sac wins. Fair enough?"

"Fair," Buddy and Matt agreed at the same time. Matt had had his head shaved and his ears were pierced with small hoops in each. His father had done his hair in the middle of the night because he said he was sick of his kid looking like a fag. I had liked his long hair. Looking like a girl was cute on a boy, I thought. But now it was shaved and he looked like a neo-Nazi, Victor had said.

Atop our skateboards, I felt the numbness in the back of my head where dumbass had just pulled my hair. I wanted to wreck him on his skateboard more than win the two cans of chewing tobacco. I knew, however, that if I wrecked Luke, he would kill me and then I would have to explain to my family that it was my fault that I was in heaven and that I had gotten there under bad pretenses. I gave the idea up after I thought that one out.

"Re-e-eady, s-e-t—GO!" The bark of Matt's last word paralyzed me for a second and I couldn't move. All three took off with swinging arms and right feet pounding the pavement while their left feet steadied their boards. Someday was running like a wounded soldier. My stomach dropped and I put my head down. The ground seemed to rise up to me and I started to paddle the street with my foot to catch up.

My wheels screamed and I bent my knees as I found enough speed to put both feet on my board. I hunkered down and began to catch up while a green queasiness began to squeeze my throat. The road had pitted dips and then smooth, pebbled roughs. *Harder*, I thought. *Push harder, harder—push the board harder.* I could hear Luke yelling in the air that my dog was a r-e-ee-tard. I went harder till the blinders began to emerge from the sides of my eyes and all I could see was the end of the cul-de-sac and the basketball net where I shot everyday. There was an uncertain pressure on my hips and legs. Then a flash of something—a shadow eclipsed my vision.

The warm June wind stung my face while a pickup truck moved to the edge of Stoney Creek Road going faster than my skateboard but slower than the three amigos ahead of me. The four of us chased the setting sun and the ultimate goal: two cans of Skoal. Two cans of Skoal would allow us spitting contests through the Fourth of July.

Through the wind I thought I could hear my brother calling, *"Ollie ollie, in come free."* I could see my mother peeling carrots by the kitchen sink and my father—I couldn't see him.

The steam from the rocky tarred pavement rose up and I let the tips of my fingers touch the sides of my board. I was going a million miles an hour.

I remembered hearing it.

"Jesus, Mary and Joseph!" The lady driver yelled then jammed the brakes on her truck. The truck hissed like polecat. Then the front wheel clipped the back of my skateboard and I catapulted off and hit the base of the basketball hoop with most of my appendages, head and

torso. My skateboard landed in Mr. Wilson's bushes thirty yards away. I rolled over and laid on my back and gazed at the sky. As if sensing something was terribly wrong and thinking someone might be in big trouble, Luke, Matt and Buddy jettisoned their skateboards and ran away.

Time was still and then in slow motion. Fur grazed my legs. Then Someday arced around me and then laid down by my side; she licked my paralyzed legs. She put her head on my stomach while the warm blood from the cuts began to bubble and drizzle from, I was certain, my severed veins. The next thing I knew, there was a dark-haired woman in a tank top staring down at me. The lady driver, I presumed. I had lost the cans of Skoal—crap. My head was pounding.

"Holy shit, girl," she said, kneeling down. Her short dark, curly hair blocked the sun. "I almost killed you."

"Quit cussing, Jenny." I heard this from a second woman slamming the truck door shut. "It's bad enough you almost killed her. You don't need to shout at her. It wasn't her fault."

Suddenly I was feeling nothing then everything at the same time. The outside of my skin was on fire. I wiped Someday's drool away with my bloodied knuckles and then pushed at her to get away from me. Then the second lady was staring at me. A green queasy feeling welled up in my stomach and I thought for sure I'd puke all over their shoes.

"Hey, there," the second one said, "are you okay? You gave us quite the scare." They were both hovering over me.

The stupid stick had hit me for sure. Now, I knew why I was in the slow math class. I couldn't speak or calculate anything—especially rate. Rate. The board was too slow and so were the words that could not form on my lips. I sat up. The two of them leaned down. The curly-haired one touched my head and I jerked away.

"It's okay," she said. "It looks like you've hit the shit out of your head, though—"

The other one shoved her. "I told you to watch your mouth, Jenny!"

"Well, God damn to the Sodomites, Andrea! Can't you see she hit the crap out of her head?"

The Andrea lady stood up from where they were both hovering over me and pushed Jenny away from me. She put her hands on her hips. "I've got a first-aid kit in the back of the truck. Jenny, grab it for me, and while you're at it, get a water bottle out of the front." When Jenny walked away, Andrea leaned in close to me. "What's your name, hon?" She reached for my head again. This time I did not jerk so much.

"Piper," I managed.

"Well, Piper. My name is Andrea and that foul-mouthed fool over by the truck is Jenny. Do you live near here, Piper?"

I nodded.

"Well, maybe we can get you fixed up." She pulled a cell phone from her hip. "What's your mom's number, Piper? I think we should give her a call and let her know you've gotten a little banged up. Do you live close?" She opened her phone.

I pointed to the end unit where Victor was probably drinking beer with Crazy Clover and playing cards.

"Is this your dog?" Jenny was back with the first-aid kit before I could tell Andrea that my mom was dead, not to mention my dad and my brother. I looked down at the cuts on my knees.

"Her name is Someday," I said.

"Someday?" Jenny asked then looked at my dog who had only three good legs and was slobbering out half of the Mississippi River out of her mouth. I was embarrassed suddenly. "Hey, Someday!" Jenny patted her on the head and scratched her rabbit ears. Someday whined and licked her arm.

"Well," Andrea said, "at least someone likes you, Jenny." Andrea was skinny and blond and very pretty. "This is Piper and we are just getting ready to call her mom to let her know we've got an injured skateboarder on our hands. What's your number, hon?"

"I . . ."

The screen door to the front of my apartment opened and Crazy Clover stepped out with Victor. Both had beers in their hands.

"P-i-i-i-i-i-p-er!" my grandfather yelled at me and stepped down from the porch. His belly was hanging over his pants. He yelled my name again and began a sober stagger toward us.

Andrea stood up. Jenny scratched Someday on her ears and I saw that Andrea had reclipped her phone to her shorts. Then Jenny gently poured some water over my head to see where the cuts were. She put the palm of her hand under my neck to cradle it and looked into my eyes. A tear ran down my cheek, over my chin, and then across my neck. My stomach arched up. I wasn't breathing right. She reached with her other hand to smooth my hair. "Hold still," she had said and that it wouldn't hurt at all. I closed my eyes for a second to feel the coolness of the water trickle through my sweaty head and then some got swallowed up in my left ear. I turned my head and saw Victor.

"Get up, girl. What's wrong with you?" His dirty hand reached for me and he pulled me up by my arm. "Well." He looked me up and down. "Who won? Looks like Luke and your other boyfriends got the best of you today."

I looked at him squarely. "They aren't my boyfriends." I breathed funny again like my whole chest would blow up. Crazy Clover stepped off of the curb and asked Andrea and Jenny if they wanted a beer.

"She may need some stitches in her knee." Andrea pointed.

"Yeah, and her head may need to be examined," Jenny said. She put her hand on top of my head. "You okay, Piper?"

Victor bent down and looked at me. "Ah, hell. She don't need no examination. We all know she and that dumb dog here are slow. Right, Clover?" Clover nodded and smiled and sipped his beer. "How much do those examinations cost anyway? You think it's worth a trade-in on your skateboard for a trip to the doc-in-the-box? Huh?" He was leaning down and staring at me.

"You all just leave me alone." I took Someday by the

collar and stomped to the grass where I thought my skateboard had landed. I could hear all of them discussing stitches, concussions and whatever else. My right knee throbbed and I was sick to my stomach. I glanced over at Clover. His right eye was freakishly pointed down and toward his nose. Tears began to well up again in my eyes. Humiliation—and strange guilt—choked me. Looking for air, my body convulsed, and then through the azalea bushes, I found my skateboard. I tucked it under my arm like I was carrying a schoolbook and headed home with Someday.

Inside the apartment, I went to my room and laid down on my bed. After a few minutes, I got up and when I looked out my window, I saw Jenny and Andrea get back in the truck and pull closer to the row of apartments. I fingered the necklace on my desk as I watched Jenny jump out and flail her arms right and left and call, "Whoa. Stop there." Andrea parked it and got out and handed Jenny a water bottle then touched Jenny's side near her hip. There were seventeen boxes of all shapes and sizes, four pictures, three lamps with no helmets on them, a large mirror and a queen-sized bed. It dawned on me right then and there that they were moving in three doors down. The unit had been empty for quite a while.

Someday moaned and laid sideways on the hardwood floor. Clover and Victor made their way back in through the front door, and then I heard the screen door slam as they both walked out the back. Then the keys turned in Clover's car. I was sure they were going to the Curbside Café two miles away to play pool and drink beer.

Patting Someday's head, I told her it was all right, girl. My head throbbed, so I laid down on the bed and listened to Someday pant as the window fan whirred in the haze of June's evening breeze.

After a good while, Someday stopped panting and put her head on my belly and the honeysuckle from her fur wafted into my nose and I slept.

Chapter 3

I awoke early the next day—Saturday. Saturday meant the pool, diving, and going to my fort.

Peering out my window, I noticed that Andrea and Jenny's truck was parked about fifty feet from my basketball net. I think fifty feet was about right—although it could have been fifty yards. I wasn't too clear on the difference. Then, limping to the back of the apartment, I stopped and stared at Victor laying on his four-poster bed in the same clothes he had on the night before. His fishing cap was on the top of his bare foot; his other foot was on the floor. Down at the hall window I looked out at the apartment pool to see if Chad, the lifeguard, was there. Yes! Pool open. My dad had thought that swimming, besides reading, was one of the most important activities in the world. I wanted him to include skateboarding and getting puppies but he just laughed at me. I remembered him teaching me how to read. At first I was slow at it. He would say, "This is *O*, Piper. Pay attention. *O* then *F.* It looks like *off* but it's like an *OV* sound. *Ov* is *of. Ov* is *of. U-u-u-V-h.* Got it. You need to memorize it. Now, read this." I heard his voice but could not see his face. He kept saying to read this, to read that, but all I wanted to do was be outside.

Immediately I walked as stiff as a board back to my room and put on my suit and soccer shorts and tank. My body was sore but I knew a swim in the pool would be good for me. I leashed Someday. We both hobbled out the back door by the four perfectly hung Norman Rockwell plates my mother and I had hung on Victor's wall two Christmases ago. They were right above the kitchen table where a smaller picture of a daisy and a sunset hung by a small nail I had tapped in for her. It said, "Bless this House."

My bare feet hit the warm pavement. Tippy-toeing the football-field-sized distance to the pool. I practically had to drag Someday the whole way.

"Come on, Someday!" I pulled. "You're slowing me down."

She picked up the pace as I yanked her collar. I had forgotten to feed her and me, I thought.

In my head, I had all kinds of crazy thoughts. Like that stupid random thought about my dad and a word I couldn't figure out. Why they put an *f* on a word that needed a *v* sounded pretty dumb to me. I was sure I was the only one in the world who had weird fleeting thoughts. The strangest things would pop right on in at the weirdest moments. Like, sometimes I would think about the time in first grade when I wasn't very nice to my neighbor's kittens where I used to live up on Carey Brook Hill, not far from Victor's. I thought about how I had scared them with yelling at them and yanking them and pushing and pulling on them too hard. I did it when no one was around. One day, I threw a couple in the prickly bushes pretty hard. I held one up and then let it go to watch it hit the ground. I had wanted to kill them and love them at the same time. I secretly crouched around where they would come around and then I would grab one by the neck and pick it up and coyly love on her, then I would shove her into the bushes like I was a diabolical serial killer or something. Then after I did it, I felt sorry I had done it and wanted to make up with them. My criminal activity went on for weeks. The kittens grew and finally became knowledgable enough to understand that I was the enemy. The back of the bushes became their home and I couldn't catch them.

It was the worst thing I had ever done. The worst thing, perhaps, I would ever do.

I felt ashamed of myself. Hurting the kittens is why I don't have my mom and dad and brother anymore. The church and my English teacher taught cause and effect. I hurt the kittens: cause. My mom, dad and brother all die at the same time: effect. No question. The men in Sunday school when my parents were alive had taught me all about Jesus and sins and penance and the Lord's Prayer. But it was all muddled up in my head with the kittens. "Fruit of thy womb Jesus" just made me think of bananas and grapes in the manger with the Virgin Mary. I knew what penance was, though. Paying the price for your sins. Hurting the kittens made my family go away. My covenant with me was to make sure that I never hurt cats again; and, to pay any price, I had to never cause anyone's death again.

It would be hard, but someone had to do it. This was not a crazy thought but a mission. I knew what that was, too.

I tied Someday to the pole next to the pool under a pin oak tree. Without even asking, the lifeguard brought over a Cool-Whip container of water and put it near her. Someday looked at him then at me and put her head down.

"She's a cool dog," Chad said. "Hey, what happened to you?" He looked at my wounded puss of a body.

"Skateboardin'," I said. "I lost the bet."

"What was the bet?" he asked.

"I dunno," I lied and shrugged. The flies were already after Someday.

"Well, if you don't know what the bet was, then it probably wasn't worth losing." He smiled then went back through the gate of the fence.

Chad was nice, I thought. I had been swimming circles around him and his small lifeguard stand since the pool opened Memorial Day. He went to Fremont High School and was a senior, I'd overheard him say to some ladies.

I looked over to the third unit in our row of apartments. Each apartment had a stoop and a small grill off to the side. You could practically hop, skip or jump to most of the porches. There were large boxwood bushes in between each porch—to give some greenery to it—I had remembered my dad saying one time.

I did not see Andrea or Jenny but wondered what they were up to with the mess they had brought in from the truck. My knee was swollen, so I got into the cool water and floated and gazed at the sky. Chad and me were the first ones there and it was quiet. The dullness in my head slowed and the chlorinated water flowed into my ears and shut the world out so all I could hear was my own internal echo and humming. It was a hollow sound, repetitious and natural-sounding.

I drifted dreamily and went forward six years in my mind. When I pulled my head out of the water, I would be eighteen and I would walk the two miles to the Curbside Café and ask for a job waiting tables, and me and Someday would live in another apartment complex. I would make hot dogs for breakfast and finally have my own computer and iPod, and I could sit and listen to my own music and make pancakes at midnight if I wanted. It was a good plan. I could do it. All I had to do was wait six years. I would have to calculate the number of days and weeks to my job as a waitress and my own apartment with my own dog.

The math was too hard in my head. I would have to use a calculator.

Later, I thought.

I pulled my head up and was still twelve. I glanced back at the third unit. Still no signs of them.

When Luke and Buddy and Matt showed up at the pool spitting Skoal all the way, I emerged from the water and, sopping wet, slipped through the gate, untied Someday and limped to my apartment.

They pretended not to notice me. No problem. I was used to that. *Nimrods.*

Grabbing some shortbread cookies from the cabinet and some bottled water, I would sneak away to my fort in the woods behind our cul-de-sac. A TV was on upstairs. A car race, it sounded like.

I had built my fort with a few pieces of old plywood I had found near the Dumpster. Nothing was really nailed together, so I had slid the edges of torn ply board and scrap wood from the dock through a gauntlet of low-lying rocks I had picked up on the shoreline. The roof of my fort sat atop two large boulders that were side-by-side. It looked more like a fort-cave than an actual honest-to-goodness fort. I made a sign that said, "Beware of the Dog," and put it right near where Someday would lay. There were three magazines: one about skateboards, another about Hollywood celebrities and a *Reader's Digest.* My English teacher had given me a book called *To Kill a Mockingbird,* but it had sat in the corner unnoticed ever since I had built the fort. On my calendar, I marked off Thursday, Friday and now Saturday. Exactly where I was.

Putting the cookies and water to the side, I took a cigarette out of a Marlboro pack Victor had left sitting on the coffee table. I put the tip in my mouth and thought of how my father had taught me to smoke when I was only five years old. I had been caught behind the woodpile of a neighbor's house where I had recently become a smoking pyromaniac. He found me with a cigarette hanging off of my lip. I looked at him and smiled and had said, "Look, Dad." I blew into the cigarette and made the end glow like a fire stick. Smoking for me was a large exhale—no inhale. I flicked it with my middle finger like I had seen my dad do and was proud that I was making him proud at my smoking abilities. At five, smoking was a difficult occupation. I was a champ. Who cared about words and reading?

He had taken me home and we sat around the kitchen table for a good while. I remembered a sinking feeling in my belly but was not sure why and what for. My dad lit me a cigarette and told me to inhale "like a dinosaur in heat." I did not know what that meant, but dinosaurs were big, so I sucked at the end of that cigarette with all my might and when I began to choke, spit and cough some assorted organs out, including my two big toes through my nostrils, he advised me to quit.

I quit smoking till I was eight or nine. Then when everyone took off for heaven, I did not care about lung cancer or throat cancer or how gross any of it was. A smoke was a smoke. And that was that.

So, Someday and I laid around and smoked a while. I picked up the *Mockingbird* book, looked at the cover and put it back down. I flipped through *Skateboarding* and looked at the flips and the tricks that were hip and in.

When I looked back at the calendar, I thought, six

more years. The calendar only went through January of the next year.

By that time, I would be in seventh grade, I thought. I smoked two more cigarettes, and then me and Someday went down by the pier where we first found each other just a few years earlier. I imagined my mom standing next to me. Her ghost and me skittered rocks against the water for a long while, then I went home to see if Andrea and Jenny were around. My head felt like the world sat right on top of it. My sore knee slowed me up and I actually had to follow Someday down the narrow path.

When I emerged from the other end of the thicket, Chad saw me and told me to come back to the pool. I did. He gave Someday some more water and then we tossed a Frisbee across the water. We didn't say anything to each other. That's what I liked about him—he wasn't complicated. When his girlfriend showed up, we stopped playing Frisbee and he ate the lunch she had packed for him.

Someday and me went home. The apartment was empty, as usual. I longed for something, I didn't know what. So, I made a cheese pizza in the oven and gave half of it to Someday. I flipped pieces into her slobbery mouth. She snatched them from the air. I swallowed a large piece then put my hand over her midget paw and rubbed it. *Good girl.*

Someday drank from her near empty bowl and I finished a flat Sprite I'd left on the counter the night before.

I took a whole carton of Goldfish to my room after

we ate the pizza—dessert. Popping them in the air to me first, then popping them to Someday—we ate thirty-three Goldfish apiece before I stopped the insanity.

When we were done, my eyes got heavy: cause.

We went to sleep together: effect.

Chapter 4

Just when I least expected it.

"Yo, Piper!" Someone was calling my name as I came out of the shadowy tree line of my private fortress in the woods behind the cul-de-sac. After our afternoon nap, Someday and I had gone back for a smoke and I skittered some more rocks. Someday rolled around in an entire bush of honeysuckle. Silly dog.

It was Jenny, the zealous cusser. I liked her already.

I waved, then looked to see if anyone else was around. Coast clear.

"Hey," she said and waved me over to where she was standing by a mail truck. She was wearing some type of uniform but I couldn't tell what it was. Someday lumbered along with me then laid down by the basketball net in her usual spot. When I got close, Jenny turned and I could see it was a postal uniform. "How are you feeling, Piper? Andrea and I talked about you earlier."

"Okay." I looked down at my feet and my dirty shoes, silently glad someone was thinking of me. I glanced at Someday.

"Well, you looked like hell yesterday. I thought that the skateboard Nazis had gotten the best of you." She patted the top of my head and I looked up at her.

Her teeth were even and neat and white, and her dark hair was short and curly. Blue eyes, I guessed but wasn't sure. She looked half Indian, like Pocahontas or something. Her skin was taut over her high cheekbones and her forearms were bigger than Victor's were. She must have been a model, I thought. She looked to be over six feet tall. And despite her burgeoning muscles, was skinny as a rail.

"Hey, I'm off to finish up at work. You're welcome to come down to our new place whenever. We're the newbies on the block. How long have you lived here?"

"A few years." I shrugged.

"Oh, well, then. You can show us around the 'hood." She stepped up into her truck. "Where are your folks, Piper?"

I looked at Someday. She was laying on her side. I had fed her half the box of shortbread cookies.

"Dead," I said. Uncomfortable, I kicked the rocks in front of me. I never knew what to say when people asked me this.

Jenny froze for a second, looked at her dash and then looked back at me. "Piper, I'm sorry."

"That's okay," I managed, still looking at Someday.

"When did they die?"

"They took my brother with them, too."

"They took your brother with them?"

"To heaven."

"Oh, yeah. So, then—it's just you and Victor?" she asked.

I nodded.

"Where's your grandma?"

"On the mantle." I kicked another rock.

"On the mantle?" she repeated.

Staring at her gold chain that ran along her thigh then up into her pocket, I stayed motionless. Jenny looked through her front window again. Someday got up and did a slow gait my way. She licked my leg and sat next to me.

Jenny leaned down and put her big hand on my head and looked into my eyes and said, "Well, it sounds like you've had quite the spell." I looked away then down. She patted me on the head. "I bet Someday here is just about most of your family these days besides Victor, eh?" She scratched Someday's ear. "Andrea and I have a cat. Her name is Precious Pink. Maybe you would want to come by and see her. I think she may be knocked up, but I can't tell yet. Where'd you get your dog, anyway?"

"By the creek near the river," I said.

"The one over there?" She pointed.

I nodded. I guessed that she was trying to make small

talk on account of the fact that I had lost my whole family practically.

"Well, Someday is a good girl. Aren't you, Someday?"

"She's just lame old Someday," I said. "All her legs don't work." Someday looked at me when I said her name.

"Well, it looks like she follows you all over the place. I imagine you're hard to keep up with, huh? Her short paw just gives her character. Part of Someday's charm, right, girl?" She stroked Someday's ears.

"I guess so," I said.

"Everybody's got charm. Right now, I'd say you charmed the angels yesterday with your skateboardin' prowess. One second sooner, and you and Someday . . ." She trailed off.

During our small talk, I hadn't noticed that Victor had stepped onto the porch. Jenny looked over at him and he lifted his fourth or fifth beer of the day in a silent toast to her. She nodded at him and waved.

I filled my lungs with the Virginia air and humidity that seemed to always line my cells with an extra coat of gook. I eyed Victor and felt the same green bile that seemed to come up from my stomach every time I was in the room with him. He always smelled of day-old Budweiser and his fingernails were dirty from hooking bait on fishing lines.

When him and Crazy Clover were around, they spat tobacco and talked about racing cars and how much things cost these days. Crazy Clover would say something like, "The price of gasoline is"—spit on the ground—"damn near sucking the paint off my pickup truck. Those A-rabs are robbing us blind."

Then Victor would spit like he was Clover's secret agent man and say, "Yeah, those damn A-rabs are a bunch of towel-headed assholes, they are."

Then Clover would say, "Yeah, towel-headed." It would cement their compact.

Victor had not waved back at her.

"Well, maybe I'll see you and Someday here, or around? I'll try to watch my cusswords so Andrea won't get mad at me. And, hey, I'm really sorry about your folks and your brother. I lost my mom three years ago to cancer. Cancer sucks." She touched my shoulder then got back up in her mail truck. "I've got two hundred more stops before I get off my route today."

"Two hundred," I said. "That's a lot."

"I do four hundred in all. I hate the rich bastards with all the magazines, but they do right by me during the holidays. I'm off for the Fourth of July, though. That's exciting. See you around, Piper."

"'Bye," I said. She put the truck in drive, put her hand out the window and waved backward. In a flash, she zoomed around the corner and was gone. I touched my shoulder where she had touched me—to feel it again, like she was still there. Then I thought of her hand on my head—my fat swollen head.

Victor waved me over. Someday and I reluctantly moved to the cement porch at the front of the apartment. I saw Mrs. Wilson watering her plants and picking at the weeds around her boxwoods.

Victor pulled out a Marlboro and lit it. I was hoping he couldn't smell the smoke on me.

"What you been up to, little girl?" he asked.

"Nothing." I walked past him and let Someday in the door.

"Hey, I'm talking to you." He grabbed my arm, then let go.

"Yeah, I'm listening." I could hear Someday's toenails click into the kitchen. Then I could hear her nose at the pan for water; empty again.

"Who's that girl you're talking to? She the one that helped you yesterday when you got in a train wreck?" He flicked his cigarette, took a sip of beer, then looked down the lane to the cul-de-sac. "Why don't you go on in the house and get cleaned up. Clover's coming over to watch the race."

I moved away from him then went into the apartment and up the steps to my room. Next to my dresser I stood and looked out the vacant, eye-like window to the spot where Jenny's mail truck had been. Two-and-a half seconds later, Someday came in and hopped on my bed. Sitting down next to her, I watched as the hanging heat and smoky wind stirred the leaves of the maple tree where I tied Someday up. Four hundred stops. That was a lot, I thought. I wondered what it was like driving a mail truck. The wheel being on the wrong side must have been confusing. I hoped it didn't confuse Jenny.

Then they came. The phantasms of people in my mind were suddenly dark creatures behind my head and shoulders. I looked quickly to the right to see if something was there. Then quickly, I glanced to the left to make sure. Flashing to my brother in my head, I could see him putting the red ants on top of the black ants and laughing at how the red ones smeared the blacks every time. The breadcrumbs would zoom down from overhead and, burping gleefully, he'd pour syrupy cola over them to see them drudge around then die.

I grabbed the covers then put my head in Someday's neck. The shadows went away and I felt a little trippy, like I would flip right out of my skin. I held onto Someday's fur for a minute, then let go, then I grabbed her again and put my whole head into the scruff of her neck. Crazy thoughts out of nowhere—now here they were again.

A hand went to my shoulder. Victor's.

"I told you to get cleaned up. And get that damn dog off the bed. She's stinking up the whole goddamn apartment." He pushed her down. "Now, get cleaned up."

I ran down to the bathroom and slammed the door.

"Now, don't go slamming doors, Piper. Just be glad you got doors to slam."

He made no sense.

I took a bath and when I got out, I looked in the mirror. My hair was dirty blond and my freckles made my face look like I had some kind of skin disease, there were so many. I tried to count them all but stopped at forty-two. I put my hands on my face and thought of my mother's words: "You're pretty, Piper." She'd rubbed the towel over my damp hair and told me, "One day, boys are going to see those beautiful green eyes of yours and won't be able to speak because it'll knock 'em out. You just watch. And your freckles are extra special. It's like

God kissed you extra hard in those spots and made them a rarity for sure." I knew she was just blowing me up, but it made me feel good anyway.

Clover puttered up in his blue Chevy Malibu. I looked out the window. He had a twelve-pack of bottled Budweiser beer in one hand and his guitar in the other.

After rebandaging my various cuts and scrapes and looking like a gray ghost, I got dressed. Downstairs, Victor and Clover cracked open cold beers and hollered like girls at the NASCAR race on TV. Three hours would pass before anyone would veer from couch, kitchen and bathroom.

"Come and watch some of this," Clover said to me as I came through the den. "It's fun. Come on." I sat down on the couch farthest away from either one of them. He didn't look at me because he was fixated on the cars that went around and around in a circle going a hundred miles an hour. This was the stupidest sport on earth. It had to be, I surmised. Cars going in a circle, then they'd pop a tire, then spin out of control, then they'd fill up with gas at pit stops where people had on uniforms and helmets. They weren't driving the car, I thought. Why the heck did they have on uniforms and helmets? How hard was it to put gas in a car and then spin in a circle? Skateboards were harder than that. No sense at all.

I got up and Clover smacked me on the butt as I went to the kitchen. It made me mad he did it, but I didn't say anything. *Freak*.

I grabbed my skateboard. "I'm going outside!" I yelled. Someday got half squeezed in the kitchen door but his eyes and throw his head back. When he did that you could tell his heart and soul were into it. I half liked him when he did it, even though Luke and Buddy and Matt had told me more than once he was the biggest weirdo slack-ass in the whole world.

Once, when Clover and Victor were far into their drinking and singing shenanigans, I went upstairs into Victor's room and nosed around. He had an old dresser with some glass on top. Underneath were pictures of my mom and dad and brother and me at different places. There was one of Victor and my dad when they had caught some huge rainbow trout somewhere I couldn't tell. My dad was holding the fish by the mouth and Victor was alongside my dad. In another picture, my brother and me stood in front of the Christmas tree in our house. Running my hands along the glass, I came upon a small box with a lock on it. It was open. Inside there were various items I counted: some race car ticket stubs from a million years ago; what I thought was my grandmother's diamond wedding ring; my mom's and dad's wedding rings; my brother's St. Christopher medal that didn't work (I didn't pick this one up for fear it would rub off on me); and something I hadn't seen in a long time that was stuck underneath a Bonnie Raitt ticket stub. It was a necklace my mom always wore. A cheap necklace, she had always said, but she wore it like it was worth a million dollars. Her mother-in-law, Victor's wife, had given it to her. It was a Celtic cross she had bought for my mom's graduation from high school. It had a thick clasp and she wore it every day till the day she died. I didn't know how long that was, I thought as I fingered it. How old was my mom? How old was my dad? I wondered who had taken these off of my parents. The police? The people at the funeral home? Victor? Crazy Clover?

"What are you doing?" Clover looked at me from the doorway. I hadn't heard the music stop.

I looked into those creepy sunken eyes. "Nothing."

"Looks to me like you're getting ready to steal something, huh?"

"Leave me alone." I ran past his beer breath and snotty nose and slammed my bedroom door. Slowly, he shuffled down the hallway to my door. I held my breath.

"Not for long, darling. Not for long—"

There was a long silence while I imagined his patchy, stubbly beard and cheek resting against my door, and then he went away. I shut my eyes hard and made every wish I could imagine to make him and Victor go away. *Go away, go away, go away.* I said it over and over in my head. I wanted them to die but knew it went against every thread of the mission and compact I had made with myself after my family died. No more hurting anything because that's what made people go away. I summoned Someday to my side and leaned into her and said, "It's all right, girl. Don't be afraid, Someday. Everything's gonna be all right." I squeezed her neck and she licked my face and nose.

We slept with my window open. An open window would make a great escape, I imagined.

In my dream I rose up above the apartment complex, my hands and arms spread out and up. I flew up and then was down again in my old house. Mom was napping on the couch beside our bay window. I sat next to her and stroked her face. A shadow of Someday laid on the floor beside her.

My mom stayed still but I knew she was alive. The cross flipped backward against her chest, her white linen. I could almost smell her.

In the middle of the night, I woke up and walked to my window. I saw Andrea and Jenny's truck parked near my hoop. Iridescent light swathed the chrome wheels. I stared at it for a long while and then crawled back into bed.

I longed for my mother, thought of a sad song and then asked Someday to hop on the bed. She did.

Good girl.

July written over top.

I counted. There were sixteen picnic tables, two kegs of beer sitting in barrels of ice and six grills cooking hotdogs, hamburgers and corn-on-the-cob. Chad, the lifeguard, and his girlfriend were overseeing most flipping of the food while several women in the crowd announced when the egg toss and potato sack races would be. The first year, Buddy and I got first place in the egg toss, but last year I'd come in dead last because the girl I did it with made me nervous and I dropped the egg on the first pitch. That same girl was here again, but I looked at her from afar and stayed my distance. Luke and Buddy and Matt and I walked around together espying the food and holding onto our skateboards. For some reason, I was okay to hang around them today. Fickle boys, but I didn't care. Buddy asked me once if he could carry my board. I looked at him funny and he didn't ask again.

I happily stared as Jenny and Andrea set up a booth for Tarot card readings. Andrea had a large, purple, cone-shaped Merlin hat on with stars and half-moons. It cracked me up. I almost fell off my skateboard when I saw it. She was the "Madam of the Tarot," as Jenny had told me. Her and I had spoken four times since they nearly killed me. One time, she shot baskets with me and kicked my ass in Pig, Horse, and Around the World. I asked her how she got so good at hoops, and she told me that "repetition was the mother of skill" and that she liked gyms and hanging out with the girls. I liked that. She played at Virginia Tech on a partial scholarship till she quit because she hated the asshole coach. She heavily emphasized the "asshole" part when she said it. (I told her I wouldn't tell Andrea she was cussing in front of me.) He had wanted to date half the team and Jenny said she wasn't interested. When it became a problem, she left.

Jenny took the time to show me how to hold the ball properly when I shot and then pointed out when I did it right. "There you go, Piper! That's right. Now here, give me the ball and we'll do a drill called rapid fire." Her voice was natural and deep and I was glad she was paying attention to me.

After we shot baskets, she pulled a dog biscuit out of her postal truck and gave it to Someday. "The waggiest of all wags," she would say to Someday. Someday would go on her back and show her belly and put her midget paw up. Jenny would scratch her and pull at her paw—I was always surprised that Someday let her. She was usually protective of her paw, but when Jenny was around, Someday let go.

Most afternoons, when I thought she'd be coming home from work, I would take Someday to the cul-de-sac and shoot and wait in the hopes she'd play. In the night, I got up to look at the truck. Jenny always parked it in the same spot—just under the streetlight, so I could make out the shape of the tires and the silver reflection from the front window and hood. Sometimes it was her postal truck, but most times, it was the Clipper truck, as she now called it in honor of me. Jenny was a card.

The Tarot money was going to build schools for children somewhere in Africa or something. Evidently, Andrea was pretty good, and with that crazy hat, she already had a line forming. Clover and Victor paid no nevermind to any of it and drank beer and played horseshoes. That was good enough for me.

Several teachers from my school who lived nearby came as well. The association hired them to help with all of the particulars. One of the science teachers was in charge of the fireworks, and my math teacher, Mrs. Svette, and my English teacher, Mrs. Raymond, were there setting up the chairs for the music and fireworks finale.

I watched them from around the bend of the fence near the pool.

Mrs. Svette scared the pee out of me. All I could see in my mind was her in front of the classroom staring us down and gritting her teeth till the muscles in her jaw popped out. "Repeat again," she would say. "Twelve times six is?" The second week of school last year, Frank McGraw mooed like a cow at that one and we stifled our uncontrollable hilarity. "Frank," she would grind out, "this isn't agricultural class, young man, if you even know what that means. Now, clamp it before I do it for you." Frank looked down then out at some of his comrades. Then she went in for the jugular, as she always did; it was the reputation that had preceded her. "Frank, why don't you come forward and do it on the whiteboard for us?" There was a long pause and Frank, who was a small kid, got up and went to the board. "Now, Frank," she would start. "Why don't you . . . ? Put that marker down." He dropped it on the floor. We all laughed. "Pick it up," she said. He picked it up and smiled. "Now, Frank, you come from a poor family, now don't you. Food stamps? I thought all the McGraws were on food stamps. Now, poor people always have poor minds." She was now speaking to most of the class. "Do you know that food stamps cost me and all the taxpayers out of their money? Hmm? Answer me, Mr. McGraw. Now, if you want to moo like a poor cow then go ahead. But you're going to need this math class so that one day you can count change back at the McDonald's you'll be working at to support your wife and kids so that me and mine can buy a Happy Meal and go to the country club. Oh, I forgot, Frank. You won't need to know how to make change. The computers will do it for you. I give up then. Sit down, young man, and if you interrupt this class again with your farmhouse Ronald McDonald routine, I'll make sure you get that job this summer."

Frank had cried like a sissy pants. We sat frozen, panicked. Who would be next?

Mrs. Svette was not to be messed with. Frank had taken the chance. A week later he was transferred out into Mr. Bruggeman's slower class and when we saw his empty chair, we knew that at any minute one of us could be next. Mrs. Svette meant business.

"Twelve times six, class?" she screeched.

"Seventy-two!" Carly Hasslebaum yelled. The rest of us sat numb.

"Twelve times ten, class?" Tens were always easy.

"One hundred twenty!" we yelled.

"Twelve times thirteen?"

Silence.

"Twelve times thirteen."

In our heads we fumbled with twelve times twelve and

then adding thirteen more to it? More silence.

"Class?"

"One hundred and fifty-six," fat Eddie squeaked out. Relief.

"Very good, then. Open your math books to page one twenty-four. Finish problems one through twenty-five and then turn it in to me. You have exactly twenty-two minutes."

We rifled out our papers and began to scratch our pencils with such fury and erase with such intensity that some of our papers got holes in them. I scratched a hole in my paper trying to figure out long division. I kept double-checking my subtraction but nothing added up. By the time the twenty-two minutes was up, I was still stuck on number fourteen. I would fail the classwork.

Later, Mrs. Svette handed it back to me and shook her head, pointing with her glossy, painted fingernails to my errors. She pursed her lips in such a way that I was afraid I'd be the next victim at the board with some food stamp crisis and how the taxpayers were the ones I needed to be sending my math work to.

Then, like a déjà vu nightmare, Mrs. Svette spotted me. I clamped my fingers hard into the chain-link fence.

She waved at me. "Piper." She waved again. "Piper, come here and say hello to Mrs. Raymond and me."

I reluctantly left my posse who, at the same time, skated over to the ramps to attempt the fifty-fifty slides none of us had perfected.

"Hey, Piper." Mrs. Raymond smiled at me. "How's your summer? You been having fun?"

I looked down and nodded.

"What's wrong, Piper Cliff?" Mrs. Svette interrupted. "Cat got your tongue?"

Holy cow—cats. I was mute.

Mrs. Raymond rescued me from the gritty jaw and pursed lips. "Well, Piper, I see you've been skateboarding. Is this your dog?"

"Yes," I said quietly. "Someday's her name."

"Well, hey, Someday. That's a cool name. I believe we call that an indefinite pronoun in English grammar."

I looked at Someday, who was wagging her black tail. An indefinite pronoun. I wasn't even quite sure what a pronoun was, but I knew what *indefinite* meant. She had really good hearing. *In-deaf-inite.* A noun, I think. Really good hearing.

"Yes, ma'am," I said confidently.

Someday licked Mrs. Svette on the leg and she jerked her whole body away in disgust. Someday followed her and licked her again. Mrs. Raymond giggled. I looked at her. She was really pretty and really pregnant. Her husband and her were expecting, she had told our class in the months before school let out.

"Well, Piper, enjoy the rest of the summer. You'll be a big seventh-grader in the fall," Mrs. Raymond predicted.

"And," Mrs. Svette added, "guess who you have for math again?"

"You?" I said.

Pursing her lips and staring down at me as if I were still sitting at my wooden desk in that rotten schoolroom, she said, "Yes, that's right, me. Your mom and dad's tax dollars won't go wasted this year."

With that, she walked away—long painted fingernails and all.

Stunned by the revelation, I stood in the middle of the field and watched my teachers walk toward the potato sack race participants. There were eight couples of all ages, each paired off and trying to coordinate the sacks and their legs and falling together all over each other. Crazy Clover and Victor were at the keg filling up again. Me and Someday stood in the middle of it all. *In-deaf-inite.* Someday had a gift. I looked down at her and scratched her ear. My dog was gifted. Really good hearing.

Ten minutes went by before I budged. Mrs. Svette had just altogether ruined my summer. I would not go to the seventh grade. I would be a middle-school dropout. Perhaps the Curbside Café could take me six years before my eighteenth birthday.

Jenny saw me in my trance and called me over to the Tarot booth. Me and my smart dog sauntered over, glum with the heaviness of having Mrs. Svette again.

Andrea was shuffling the cards. "Piper, you want your cards read?" She looked at Jenny and then they simultaneously looked at me.

"I don't have any money for your charity," I said. Someday hobbled to Jenny and laid down.

"That's all right," Andrea said. "I'll do you for free since I have a lull. Looks like people are fixing to eat." She adjusted her hat, which was cockeyed, and glanced at me again.

I smiled then giggled. "Okay."

Jenny winked her blue eyes at me. When she did that, it felt like an angel's wings had brushed my skin and the hairs stood up from my ankles to the top of my head.

I sat down in the chair across from Andrea, and Jenny nodded that it was okay. She must have sensed my slight recalcitrance, my slight apprehension.

"Now," Andrea said, "do you know anything about Tarot cards?"

I shook my head.

"Well, a short summary would be that they are like reading your horoscope but a little fancier. Have you ever read your horoscope?" When I nodded, she said, "Good, then you know a little already. When's your birthday, Piper?"

"December twenty-fourth."

"Wow, a Christmas baby, eh. That's cool. How old will you be on your next birthday?"

"Thirteen."

"Thirteen?" Jenny questioned. "That means you'll be in what grade?"

"Seventh."

Andrea shuffled the cards then asked me to give her my hands. I put both of my hands on the table for her to hold. She put my hands together, then cupped her hands around them. "Seventh grade," she said as she held my hands. "I remember seventh grade. That was an interesting year." She paused and put her head down as if she were in prayer.

I watched her hands around mine. I didn't want her to let go. She must have felt something in me because she held them for quite a while, and when she squeezed them as a sign she was done, I looked her in the eyes and she looked at me. Connected.

"You're beautiful, Piper. Has anyone ever told you that you have the most beautiful eyes?"

I was frozen to the chair and my face got hot. Jenny noticed my discomfort and nudged Andrea, "Come on, Andrea. Let her shuffle the cards, for Christ's sake. Don't you see this girl's got to go skateboarding and show those fool kids that she can nollie-ollie the heck out of them?"

Jenny knew what a nollie was. I couldn't believe it.

She handed me the cards and I shuffled them like she had shown me. When I was done, I handed her the cards.

"Now," Andrea said, "we're going to do three cards then a bonus fourth card reading." She spread the deck out across the lip of the table till they looked like a long straight fan of cards. "Pick three cards and turn them over in front of you first." I did.

"Shit," Jenny barked out.

"Jenny, for the love of God, quit your cussing in front of her."

"Sorry."

"What's wrong?" I asked.

"Nothing, except for Jenny's rotten mouth. Don't pay attention to her, Piper." She looked over the three I had pulled. "You have gotten three interesting cards. The first one is the four of cups. The second here"—she pointed—"is the Empress, and the last one here is the Tower. The first one is what we call a minor card and the last two are soul cards. Now, with all of that in mind, it looks as if we need to go ahead and pick your fourth card to see what the outcome is going to be. Go ahead and pick the outcome card."

All of the pictures looked weird to me, especially the Tower card, which showed fire and mountains and open windows and people with crowns falling from the sky and lightning bolts and open windows with flames. I slowly reached for the last card and tenuously turned it over. The World, it said at the bottom. It had a naked woman in the middle with a big green wreath around her.

"My granddaughter doesn't do this voodoo shit." *Blam.* Victor grabbed the top of my arm. "I don't know what you two girls are trying to do with this hocus-pocus—"

"Mr. Cliff," Jenny said, "we're just having fun. Andrea is raising money to help build schools for children in Africa."

He pulled me off the stool and then let me go. Someday got up and came near me, brushing against me. I teetered back, fell in the dirt.

"Get up, you clumsy fool," he barked at me.

I jumped up and stood behind him and watched. Clover sipped his beer at the side of the booth where he'd been leaning. He hesitated for a fraction of a second, then made his move.

"Look here, Victor"—he slapped the World card—"they got pictures of naked women in this deck. Women holding cards with naked women seems a little queer to me. What do you think, Victor."

"Hey, asshole, they're Tarot cards. And it's a good cause." Jenny swooped the cards up and put the deck back together. "Schools for children. Are you familiar with the concept of school?"

"Jenny," Andrea admonished her, "watch out." But Jenny didn't look at anyone but Clover. Someday licked me and I told her to stop.

Clover pushed his crooked hat up on his head and his gappy smile showed unbrushed teeth. His crazy eye had a film of mucous over it that I could barely look at without getting the heebie-jeebies. He put his wet cigar to his mouth and said, "I know what you two are. Looks like we got some alternative folks in the neighborhood, Victor. What do you say?"

"Sure looks that way. Piper, you and Someday go to the pool."

"I don't want to go," I said.

"Let her stay, Victor," Andrea said nicely. "She's having fun. We aren't doing any harm. It really is for a good cause. No hocus-pocus, I promise." She was trying to cajole the oldest fart in the neighborhood. "She got some really good cards . . ." It was her last attempt before Victor launched into his monologue of Victorisms.

"The only playing cards I know about have numbers and four suits: spades, diamonds, clubs and hearts. You can play old maid, crazy eights, rummy and poker. Normal playing cards for normal playing people. Kings and their queens, and if you're lucky, a good spread every now and again. Now, Piper here has been through a lot these last few years and she doesn't need you two coming along and filling her head with nonsense. Next thing I know she'll be wanting a tattoo and a belly button ring. Now, she's not much to look at, but she's all I got and I don't want her doing these cards. I am her only guardian left and what I say is the law of the land. She goes to church, she goes to school, and she's got this smelly dog—and me and Clover here. He's her godfather. Do you all know what God is, since we've been asking questions about school and all?"

Jenny looked like she was going to have an aneurysm. Andrea began to shut down her operation.

Victor looked at me. "Now, go on, Piper." He gave Someday a shove with his shoe.

Jenny looked at the both of them and said, "Oh, for Christ's sake, Clover, why don't you loan Victor here your guitar and have him sing us a ballad. Perhaps 'Crimson and Clover' can be you all's theme song. You guys seem pretty tight and all. What do you say, Andrea?"

"Fuck you!" Clover spit on the ground. "Damn carpet munchers."

"You two stay away from Piper, you hear?" Victor pointed his finger in Andrea's face.

Jenny moved in. "You and Clover here have a nice Fourth of July, now," she said. "Make sure you eat plenty and get a good base of food in your guts." She rubbed her belly. "You're both going to need it for all the beer and how you'll pass out on each other later."

Clover grabbed her shirt by the sleeve then let go. "Watch your mouth before I have to—"

Jenny pushed him away. "Get your slimy hands off of me, you Shrek-headed pig toe."

"Stop it, you two." Andrea stepped forward. "It's a holiday. Let's try and not make our own stupid fireworks over a few cards and—"

"Stay away from her." Victor glared at me, then shifted his stony eyes to them.

With wings on my feet, I flew away from all of them as fast as I could. Past the pool, I dodged Chad and his girlfriend. I heard Buddy yelling my name to come to the ramps. Jenny yelled for me and ran my way but stopped. When I looked back, Andrea was taking her cone hat off and Clover was looking my way. There was only air between me and the ground I floated over. I felt guilt, shame, curiosity—all at the same time. Victor's pompous speech had embarrassed me right when I was having a good time.

By the time I reached my fort, I was out of breath with the running and the craziness of it all. My lungs heaved for air and I kicked everything that was kickable. I kicked the plywood then kicked the maple flag right off the pole. My shoes slid on the dirt and I kicked up all my magazines and the dumb book my schoolteacher had given me. Everything became kickable and everything landed in a pile all over the sodden floor. Someday barked at me, and I stopped then suddenly and wished I could wash my freckles away and Victor with them.

Then Someday and me laid down and I looked up and watched the black sparkling sky. Suddenly, I could hear my dad's voice. *Piper, come down here. I want to show you something. Come here, Pipe.* But I couldn't go where my dad wanted me to go because my legs had heavy tar in them and my mouth was immovable. Mute.

I counted seventy-eight evening stars, then let go of the innumerability of it all and closed my eyes.

Chapter 6

The moon's luminous glow settled over me like a blanket as I floated in sleep for a good while. Images of my mom and dad and brother dallied in my mind. I greeted their ghosts with a smile, languid lurid apparitions in the cloak of night. In the distance, I thought I heard some footsteps, but in my dreamy fog, I couldn't make them out. I reached over to make sure Someday was still there. She was. Eventually, I awakened from my mind's misty veil to try and reason with the happenings of the early evening's affairs. Just when I opened my eyes and glanced up, a large, prodigious figure towered over me.

Clover.

Fear seared through me, up and down my legs and

spine like a million spindly spiders. I could not make out his face but in the moonglow saw a filament of light catch the crazy eye that was extra glazed from a million beers.

"Where you been, Piper?" he slurred. "Your granddaddy and I been looking for you last little bit?" He swigged on another beer and staggered.

I grabbed a hunk of Someday's fur. He was right in front of my fort and hovering over me. My stomach felt green and my head was red hot. I quickly surveyed for a route to take or a weapon to ward off his nastiness. The hardest thing in my fort was the *Mockingbird* book. I slid my hand behind Someday, groped, then grabbed it.

"Nice fort you got here. What do you and your dog do here all day long?"

"Read some," I said. "That's all."

"Read? Read some? Read some?" He mocked me and got louder the more he slurred and tried to enunciate.

If I moved now, he would get me. I sharpened my squint on him and squeezed the book in my hand. Someday sat up.

"Reading's for sissies," he said. "Now, you don't want to be a sissy now, do you, Piper?" With that, he sat down just to the left side of me, his hip and his thigh touching mine. He sipped his beer and looked out at the creek. "All that reading will make you soft in the temple." He touched my temple with his cheesy finger. I jerked my head away. "Aww, now, that didn't hurt, did it?"

"No," I said. I had my right hand firmly on the book.

He traced the outline of my face with his finger all the way down to the corner of my lip. "Now, little miss, you and me, we're gonna have a good time. I promise not to hurt you if you promise not to scream or tell. Understand. Victor's real upset with you right now, and if he found out you been fooling with me, he might give you away. He might give you up. He might take your dog away. Now, we wouldn't want that to happen, now would we?" He leaned across me and put his hand on my thigh and gripped it hard. "You understand, don't you?" He began to slide his hand up my leg and then lowered his head to put his gnarly, chapped lips onto mine.

Just then, fireworks began to explode like a million calliopes in the sky, bursting everywhere. Clover jerked from the noise.

From my stomach and lungs and all the way up through the roots of my burning throat, I screamed. "You s-o-o-o-o-o-o-o-o-n-n-n-n-n-n o-o-o-o-o-f a b-i-i-i-i-i-i-i-i-i-i-tch!" Jenny had taught me how to cuss good. With the corner of *To Kill a Mockingbird,* I rammed it six or seven times, I wasn't sure, as hard as I could into the middle of his sickening eye. We scuffled. Someday barked. I kept jamming it and jamming it till he let go and put both of his hands over his pockmarked gin-blossomed face. Clover spat at me then stumbled over the flagpole I'd kicked earlier. I leapt up, got out of his reach and began running through the woods. Branches and limbs slapped at me and my foot hit a stump and I fell down. *Get up. Get up.* I ran and ran and ran through the thicket of the trees. There were footsteps behind me.

One. Two. Three. How many? Clover was yelling and screaming at me. There was a whoosh and a whimper and a frightening squeal.

I floated. No sound. No noise. The sky lit with red, white and blue. The explosions in the sky were in sync with my heart. Rapid. Rapid. Rapid. It kept beating. Mrs. Svette yelled, "Three times ten." I couldn't answer. I wasn't sure. I kept running and crying and sweating and not feeling and not feeling. Surely, Clover was three steps behind. *He's right behind me.* My mom was talking to me about freckles and dad was hooking bait on a fishing line for my brother, Jack. I clenched the sides of my head. My body created a wake through the woods. I could feel him on me. The heat. The breath. The grip. *I'm going to die. This must be it. I'm going to die with Clover's spit on my face.* I wished he was dead. I killed him. I killed him. I killed him with a book about a bird.

Someone grabbed my hand.

"Piper? Hey . . ." It was Jenny. "Where have you been? We've been looking all over for you."

I looked at her and then to the line of apartments on the other end of the creek. Andrea was there with Precious Pink in her arms. The pregnant cat.

I fainted.

• • •

"Come on, little girl." I could hear Jenny's voice inside my ear. Her arms were under my legs and back. She carried me. How, I don't know. But I was off the ground and into her arms.

Through the fog of my mind, while the bombs were still bursting in air like the faint song humming in my head, I could hear my mom's voice. It wasn't clear but it was there. I smelled honeysuckle. I smelled White Shoulders perfume, like my mom used to wear. I looked up at Jenny, who had pulled me from the cloak of the thicket and smiled a bit. She smiled back at me and said that I was okay. I pressed my head into her chest and felt the *drum-drum* of her own heart murmuring to me. Andrea moved ahead of us toward their apartment.

"Did I kill him?" I asked.

"Did I kill him?" Jenny repeated. "What do you mean?"

"Clover?"

"Did you kill Clover?"

"Yes."

"Was Clover bothering you, Piper? What happened in the woods?"

I stayed quiet. I remembered his words in the woods. I could see the celestial sky light up with the streaking colors of the freedom night. Then the blaze of downward spirals and arcs—how the sky fell silent like me. A stray firecracker or two began to take over on the sidewalks where Buddy and Luke and Matt were probably still ticktacking around on their boards.

Andrea held the front door open while Jenny carried me through. Once inside, Andrea shut the door and began dialing numbers on her cell phone.

"Who are you calling?" Jenny asked.

"Lucy McGillicutty," Andrea said.

"Why her?"

"Because this little girl just fainted and Lucy's the best nurse around and she can tell us what to do."

"Andrea." Jenny laid me down on the couch. "It's the Fourth of July. Lucy McGillicutty is probably hanging from the rafters at the Richmond Braves game because she's been through a barrel of beer."

"Well, maybe so, but she's the best drunk nurse I know and she always answers when I call her."

"That's because she used to have the hots for you, Ms. Sassy Pants." Jenny went into the kitchen. Andrea put the phone to her head and rolled her eyes. Precious Pink followed Jenny. Andrea looked at me and put her finger to her head and did a loop-de-loop around her temple while Jenny cussed about the fact that they were out of Gatorade.

"Lucy? Lucy?" Andrea yelled into the phone. "Lucy, it's Andrea. Hey, happy Fourth. No, no, no. I'm not alone. A T-shirt and shorts. Shut up, Lucy. Look, I have a question." She headed up the steps out of earshot.

Jenny came in with a bottle of water and sat next to me on the couch. "We'd been looking for over an hour for you. Finally, Buddy said that you might be at your fort, so we were headed that way. What happened? Why did you take off? Did Clover hurt you? If he did, then I'm going to kill him if you didn't off him already. Soon as Andrea gets back down here I'm going to go into the woods and find that son of a bitch. Oh, sorry. I didn't mean to cuss. Hell, I don't know. What happened?"

"Where's Someday?" I asked. She had not followed us from the woods.

"I don't know. She was with you?"

I nodded. Suddenly, I became catatonic as the revelation hit me. She was with Clover. Then I burst into tears. Fast, uncontrollable, huge streams burbled down my face.

"Andrea!" Jenny yelled.

"What?" She was coming back down the stairs. "I'm right here. Lucy said to give her plenty of fluids and some O.J. because her blood sugar might be low. What's wrong?" She saw me crying.

"That Clover son of a—" She stopped herself. "That Clover, Piper thinks, has her dog." Andrea stood there motionless. "Well, he's got the dog and, well, it's the only thing she has that isn't either drunk or who knows what else. I'm going to look for Someday. Get her something to drink."

"But what about the cat. You can't bring that dog here, Jenny. She'll hurt the cat."

I cried harder.

"Andrea, have you seen the dog? She's not going to hurt a flea. Jesus, she can barely walk with that bad paw and all. I'm bringing her here."

Andrea nodded. "I'll put Pink in the guest bedroom. Go on. Go find Someday."

Jenny leaned down and kissed me on the cheek. "Don't worry, Pipe. I'll find her and bring her here. It'll be all right."

Exactly the same words I used with my dog. I trusted

Jenny to find her, and Andrea took care of me and talked to me and brought me juice and something to eat. She turned on the fireworks on TV and every now and again got on her cell and made a call. I wasn't sure who she was talking to and didn't care.

Suddenly, I felt shivers and the creepiness of the shadows that came and visited me sometimes. Quickly glancing over my shoulder, I half expected to see Crazy Clover standing there with blood oozing from his eye and his Budweiser in his hand and halitosis. I gripped my sides underneath the blanket and shut my eyes tight, praying my mind would not play bad games on me and scare me like so often it did. I thought of the jewelry in Victor's box—the rings, the ticket stubs, the Celtic cross my mom had worn. I saw Someday's short leash on the maple tree outside of my apartment and the dead sticky ants lying on top of the two-day-old food. Her water bowl was empty. I was sure of it. I winced, then whined.

"Hey, sweetie." Andrea took my hand. She looked like a movie star. Her hair was long, blondish red and her nose was austere—English-like in its shape. Her shoulders were square and strong and her arms thin. Her nails were painted muddy red and her voice was raspy. This was first I'd noticed her throaty, raspy voice. "What's wrong? You want to talk?"

"No, ma'am," I said.

"Andrea," she said. "Call me Andrea. Just don't cuss at me like Jenny does. Boy, does that girl have a mouth on her." We both laughed. It was the first time I had laughed in about a billion years. I'd been counting.

Andrea held my hand and I pressed mine back into hers. I longed for something in that second, like when I had floated in the pool three weeks earlier.

At four in the morning, Jenny came home. Andrea was asleep in the bubba chair and I was awakened by the sound of the door but pretended to be asleep.

"Did you find the dog?" Andrea asked.

"No," Jenny whispered, "but I did find Clover. They had to take him to the hospital. Apparently, he fell in the woods taking a pee and hit his eye on a thorny branch. It was mashed in even worse than it already was. His leg got cut really badly all the way down to his Achilles, too. Victor drove him and I told Victor we'd watch Piper till he got back. I called for Someday along the creek and then by the side of the river down to the Pony Pasture. But no luck. When daylight comes, I'll go out looking for her in the truck. I can't remember, but I don't think she wears a tag. I didn't see one on her collar."

"Was Victor cool with Piper being here after what happened with the Tarot cards and all?" Andrea asked.

"I don't think he could have given a rat's ass. He was more worried about his drinking buddy than anything. Plus he was half in the grocery bag himself."

The whispering went on for a while. Then Jenny leaned over and kissed Andrea on the lips. I counted. They kissed four times. The first two were soft and short, but the last two seemed to go on longer. I had never seen a woman do this to another woman. They weren't kissing like friends or sisters . . . they were kissing like what I had seen in the movies. Their faces were close in the light of the window and they held each other nestled up in the arms of the bubba chair.

They were good shadows in the darkness.

Waiting and watching in what would be one of many long nights, for a moment I was safe in this small apartment in Goochland County where these two women, evidently, liked each other very much. I closed my eyes and replayed their kisses in my head, losing count to sleep.

"Vermont," and in another there must have been six or seven girls all bent over in the ocean sand pushing a flag that had red and blue and violet and yellow and some other colors on it. Just below the picture, it said, "Our Iwo Jima in Va Geenia." I didn't get it. I touched the edge of one picture that had Jenny in her postal uniform by her truck. In another Andrea was holding the hand of a woman who was not Jenny.

Lying on the kitchen table were some beer caps from the night before and some loose change: fifty-six cents—a quarter, a dime, four nickels and a penny. I counted again to make sure. Andrea's Tarot cards were laying on the table, too, but I did not touch them for fear I might start something. It was bad enough there was a pregnant cat upstairs. *I cannot hurt the cat; I will not hurt that cat.* I repeated that to make sure it stuck.

The layout of their apartment was much like Victor's except everything looked cleaner and smelled better. Looking out the windows that faced the basketball net and the cul-de-sac, I wished that Someday would come out of the opening to the woods like she always did when she was following me. Lame old Someday. I thought of her paw and how it always slowed me down. *Come on, Someday. Come on, girl.* All at once I winced—my stomach and heart felt heavy and still. I pined for her here with me and Jenny and Andrea—even if pregnant Precious Pink was going to have babies. Where was she? If she was hurt, or worse, then I was sure I would die. Clover passed like an ugly phantom through my mind but I pushed him out. I had no room in my head for Clover this morning.

All I could really remember was running through the splintered woods and—

"Good morning, Pipey," Jenny yawned and smacked me on the butt.

"Hey," I said.

"Hey, what?" She lowered herself like a frog then jumped in the air. Silly.

I rubbed my butt. "Hey, watch it."

"Watch what, Pipey? I'm going to get you, little girl." She bear-hugged me and lifted me up off of the ground.

I said, "Hey, hey, hey, hey," but she didn't let go and that was okay because I liked it and laughed.

"Shut up, down there. We have a sleeping mother and a cranky girlfriend who didn't go to sleep till after five o'clock this morning!" It was Andrea.

We looked at each other, me and Jenny. She put her fingers to her lips and gave me the shush sign. I mimicked her. She winked at me and summoned me to follow. We tiptoed up the stairs ever so lightly. At the top of the steps, Jenny froze and then put her fist back behind her. The index finger out: one. Got it. The middle finger out: two. Got that, too. Then the ring finger: three. A counting no-brainer. I got it.

On three, we catapulted ourselves into their bedroom and jumped on top of Andrea. Jenny told her she had slept all week because that's all that university students do anyway—sleep, sleep, sleep, and eat chips and Ramen noodles. Andrea put the pillow over her head and said to get off of her but Jenny straddled her and tickled her sides through the covers. I giggled and then Jenny was asking me what I was giggling at and then tickled me, too. I was paralyzed with laughter. Andrea pulled the pillow off of her head and smacked Jenny on top of her head.

Jenny said, "Now, is that the way to treat your girlfriend after all I've done for you?"

By then, Andrea was stupefied by her own laughter. I laughed with her, not knowing why, but she infected me with it. We were in high giggle—all three of us. Jenny then bopped me on the head with the pillow. I fell backward on the cat, who had been laying there unnoticed. One loud meow, and my eyes must have gotten as wide as the Mississippi Delta because Andrea and Jenny just froze, giggleless, staring at me as if amber light had surrounded my head and body.

"Don't worry about Pink," Andrea said, finally. "She's a resilient one. It's hard to hurt mama."

I didn't say a word. I was scared. It was the cat scourge upon me. But, then like nothing had happened at all, Precious Pink just got up, stretched on the floor and pattered out the door and into the bedroom down the hall.

Andrea looked at me. "Well, we had a big night last night, Ms. Cliff. How are you feeling?"

"Okay. A little sore is all. Thank you."

Jenny rubbed the top of my head. "Thank you for what?"

"For carrying me here."

"Ah, shit. That wasn't anything. You're light as a feather—"

"Jenny, if you cuss one more time around Piper, I'm

going to kick you to the curb!"

"Well, God durn, poo-poo, freak, butt and breasts. Is that better?"

"Yes, it is. Now move—both of you. I have to go to the bathroom."

"You mean take a piss? Don't listen, Piper. She gets real feisty when I start talking smack."

"I don't care. You don't say anything that Victor don't say."

"How is it living with him anyway?" Andrea asked. "He treat you okay?"

"Yeah. I suppose so. It's different than when Mom and Dad and Jack were around—"

Jenny stopped me. "Jack was your brother?"

I nodded. "Yeah. When we lived on the hill, I never really saw Victor except for when he came up in his truck to take them fishing—"

"Who fishing?" Andrea asked. She got out of the bed and stretched.

"Jack and Dad. They went fishing every Sunday practically and never took me. I complained sometimes but then Mom and me would do something together. She liked the movies. So, a lot of times we'd go see a *Harry Potter* or a cartoon—like, we saw *Finding Nemo* once. My favorite fish was Dorey. She cracked me up 'cause she never knew what was going on. Then after a while, my dad and mom and me and Jack started hanging out by the river on evenings after the fishing was done. Mom would drive me there because she knew I had felt left out." I stopped for a second and lost my train of thought then said, "I think the last one we saw before she died was—I can't remember."

"When did they die?" Jenny asked.

"About two years ago. I was at home with Someday."

"Speaking of Someday . . ." Andrea glanced at Jenny.

"Well, it looks like me and Pipery." She was changing her naming conventions for me right often. "It looks like me and Pipery-roo will be looking for something, somehow, somewhat, some . . . .some . . . some . . ."

"S-o-o-m-m-e-D-D-D-a-a-a-y-y-y!" I yelled at her.

"Well, you don't have to be so corrective and all, pipsy doodle." Jenny cracked me up. She was a comic.

So, after blueberry Pop-Tarts, milk and coffee, Jenny and Andrea and I headed out into the streets of the complex and neighboring woods and fields to find my lost dog. We stopped by my apartment first to tell Victor, but he was passed out in his own pee on the couch, so we left. Andrea and Jenny walked through the apartment. I thought I heard Jenny say the F word three times as she glanced around, but I wasn't sure. Andrea stopped in the kitchen and noticed a bottle of Jack Daniels nearly empty, something he drank when he was really uptight. There were flies on two uneaten hamburgers, and the dishes were soaking in muddy water in the sink. They'd been there since Thursday. Today was Monday. The laundry spilled out onto the floor from the adjacent closet that held the stackable washer and dryer. A bag of Cheetos laid on the floor where ants were having the feast of a lifetime. I was embarrassed that my new friends were witness to such disarray. Quickly, I poured soap on the dishes.

Andrea touched my back and reached over to stop me, turning off the faucet. "Come on," she said. "Let's go find your dog."

I headed to the maple tree. The empty bowls were there and the tethered worn leash tied to the base of the tree, but no Someday.

We did a once-around of our row of apartments. I saw Mrs. Wilson in her kitchen window doing dishes. She had a dish towel on her shoulder and she waved at me when I passed by. Instinctively, I waved back.

Meandering into the woods, I showed Andrea and Jenny my fort where I hung out. Only Buddy and I really knew about it, I told them. Lately, though, I thought maybe Luke and Matt had swung by, because there was a can of chewing tobacco and my Beware of the Dog sign was gone. My weapon of choice from the night before, the bird book, lay about twelve feet from where Clover had put his grubby hands on me. Andrea glanced at the cigarette butts laying snuffed out on the ground. She picked up the half-smoked pack of Marlboro Lights and shoved them into her pocket. I told her that I thought maybe other people had been there, too. She said, "Uh-huh," and walked away.

We traipsed along the side of the creek and along the path out to the James. Jenny asked me how Someday got her name and I explained to her that it was my mom's idea that we would someday get a dog. Then I remembered my sassing about it and stopped my story.

As if sensing my retarded apprehension, Andrea asked again, "How did your folks pass, Piper?" She whistled for my dog. "Come on, Someday. Hungry? Want a treat?"

"Andrea, you don't need to be bringing that up now, for cryin' out loud. She's lost her dog—"

"Someday's not lost," Andrea interrupted her. "She's just taking a sabbatical from the night of drama."

"Car crash," I stated. "S-o-m-e-d-a-y-y-y-y-y!" I yelled and grabbed at a branch that flung back and smacked Jenny in the shoulder.

"Yo, watch it there, Pocahontas. You nearly nailed one of your leaders." Jenny playfully shoved me aside. I shoved her back and Andrea told us that we were both goofy in the head.

"You're the goofy one in the head, Mrs. Study-aholic."

Andrea ignored us both and went along ahead.

For three long hours, we searched for Someday. Every so often, Andrea would call somebody on her cell phone and ask them to make a call for her to a pound or the SPCA or the Humane Society. She talked to a guy named Brock who said he was still too drunk from the night before but would help later. Then, after Lucy would not answer her phone, she said she was going to call some girl named Alma, but Jenny stopped dead in her tracks and said to call Vera. Vera, Jenny explained, lived in the next county and had been a friend for more than twenty years.

"Vera will know what to do," Jenny said. She's a retired librarian with nothing to do. She's God-durn resourceful." Jenny made me laugh again. Andrea called her, and Vera, evidently, got on it.

"If anyone can help, it's Vera," Andrea looked at us. Jenny nodded.

"Vera's good with dogs, Pipe." Jenny rubbed the top of my head. "Andrea's right—Vera will figure out a way to help. She always does."

Retracing our steps from the night before and then walking the two miles near the old house where I used to live atop of Cary Brook Hill with my parents and family, we called for Someday. Sometimes simultaneously, sometimes in one-two-three fashion. Jenny would start, then Andrea would holler, then I'd shout out, too, as I brought up the rear, like a small army. The elementary school and middle school where my brother and me went to looked older in the summer, the parking lot vacant and the heat wavering off of the two conjoined blacktops. The jungle gym looked tired from years of kids climbing and hanging, and it stood childless. The softball diamond had grass overgrown around the edges from neglect. The maintenance men were done for the year. There were no souls to be found—just locked doors and empty classrooms and chairs standing at attention on top of tables in the cafeteria window.

It began to slowly sink in that something was the matter and that Someday was nowhere to be found. I began to repeat to Andrea and Jenny the same question, "Where do you think she might be? Do you think we should go back to the woods? Where is she, you think?"

They would respond in unison, "I dunno but we'll find her." Over and over and over again.

Then, as we circled the edge of the playground, I

looked up at Jenny and said, "Do you think Clover did something to her?"

My last question was a revelation. *Of course he did*, I thought. Crazy Clover had killed my dog.

I laid down and went limp in the grass near the foot of my school's blacktop. I clacked then clenched my teeth hard and threw my arms up in the air to admonish God once and for all, once and for all, once and for all—for playing these horrible nasty Godforsaken, God-for-nothing, God-for-rotten tricks on me. Out of the castle's window on the Tower card in Andrea's Tarot deck, I could see the people flinging, jumping and then impaling themselves onto a wind of nothingness. God had caused all of this, I thought. God was to blame. God had taken everyone, and now my dog. The water bowl had been too low. Her uneaten food with the ants crawling all over it. I had left her tied to the tree for too long. What had I done? What was it? Was it the smoking? Did I cuss too much? What had I done to deserve this? I hurt Clover. That was it? Perhaps. What in the hell was I doing in church? I cried. I screamed until my neck swelled as if the fluid in every cell in my body wanted to rupture and split like nuclear fission, like an atom bomb. My body was coming unglued.

Infuriating. It was all infuriating.

Then I ran.

I ran from Andrea and Jenny all the way back to Victor's dumb-ass apartment, the dumb-ass apartment complex and my dumb-ass life. He wasn't there. I stomped up the steps, my bangs in my eyes, all the way up to his room.

Out of breath and panting, I threw open the jewelry box where my parents' rings were and the mementos from I didn't care what. One. Two. Three. Four—I grabbed the Celtic cross, opened the window and flung it out as hard as I could.

Three holes in my heart resounded. God was to blame.

Now, I had four.

"Don't you take my dog, too. Don't you take my dog, too. Don't you take my dog, too. You son of a bitch. She's lame and she needs me and she's lame. Don't you take her away, too. Don't you take my Someday, too. Someday!" I spit on the ground. "Someday!" I spit again. "You son of a bitch!" I wailed till I had no more wail in me. Then I just choked it out and choked it out. The bile came up, but I forced it back down because I still had more to say. "Don't you take her away, too." I put my head on the windowsill and drooled. My whole body hiccupped.

Mr. and Mrs. Wilson opened the door to their apartment and both, side by side, came out into the parking lot to look up at me, half incredulous. Mrs. Wilson smoothed her apron and put her hands on her hips. Mr. Wilson took his glasses off and squinted up in my direction.

"What are you looking at?" I slammed the window down, kicked Victor's bed and then locked myself in the bathroom.

Chapter 8

Three days passed like slow tar running uphill in the winter.

I moped around the pool, my apartment and my fort. I walked aimlessly by broken, worn fences and smelly trashcans and peered around every corner where I thought my dog might be. Calling her name in whispers—then sometimes I would just talk to her. "It'll be all right, Someday. We'll find you." I would say it aloud and then sometimes just in my head. I left God out of it. I was pissed at Him.

Andrea and Jenny helped look with me when they had time between Andrea's studies and Jenny's postal route. Andrea told me that her friend Vera was checking the pounds and the SPCA everyday to see if Someday turned up. I thanked them and each time I left them, I went to the pier where we used to fish, smoked cigarettes and cried. Smoking helped me breathe. I got good at lighting the cigarettes while they were in my mouth. I flicked the ashes in the water and pulled the splintered wood from the pier and threw it in the water.

Even Victor felt bad for me and made me my favorite grilled cheese and brown sugar sandwiches. It was the nicest thing he'd probably ever done for me but I did not care. I took three bites and put it back on my plate. He said he'd called the shelters but none had a dog with a bad paw and rabbit ears like Someday. I could barely hear his words.

He told me that Clover had had a pretty good fall in the woods on the Fourth and was four hours away at some eye institute. It'd be four to six weeks to get his eye working properly along with his busted leg.

I shrugged when he said this and went to my room.

I longed terribly for my dog and pressed my face into the blanket to smell her smell. Dog mixed with honeysuckle. I found some loose fur embedded in the fabric. I gently pulled them out, put them to my nose and then put them in my pocket, careful to keep the hairs annealed together.

Longing was a funny thing. I felt guilty for how I had neglected her. She was in my head. I could see her there all the time—following me everywhere, licking me, letting me hold her, barking at anything that came close. My lost buddy. Every second, minute and hour were filled with Someday. I could not and did not want to get her out of my mind. Someday was in me and I felt I was in her. The languishing was my cross to bear, I reckoned.

After smoking two cigarettes at the pier, I finally summoned the Big Guy overhead. I was pissed, but we needed to chat.

Putting my hands together and bowing my head like we were supposed to do in church, I prayed with all my might that the Taker-Away-of-all-Things would be the Giver-Back of my one thing. I wanted her back. *Please.* I wanted her back. *Please.* I said three hundred "pleases" before I stopped. Then I tried an "Our Father" and a "Hail Mary." I remembered the words to the first, but when I got to the "Hail Mary full of Grace the Lord is with thee, blessed are thou among women and kids," I forgot the rest. So I just said the first part a couple of times to try anyway. I knew that Someday was In-deaf-inite and had really good hearing. I just knew that if I called loud enough for her that she would hear me and come home. But when I opened my mouth to call, nothing came out. So, I prayed louder in my head.

I thought about the cruelty to the kittens, the mistakes I made in math, why I hadn't been in the car with my parents and brother, too. Perhaps that was the biggest mistake I hadn't counted on. I should have been in the car, too. I then promised to pay more attention to my dog and to keep her water bowl full and to give her more treats and rawhides and pets. *Please God, read my mind. Read it please, Sir.* I opened my mouth again. I looked out onto the glistening water at the end of the pier. *Our*

Father. Hail Mary. Our Father. Hail Mary. Our Father. Hail Mary.

Please, God, read my mind.

The sun was going down on me.

On day four of no Someday, Matt, Luke and Buddy banged on my screen door one late Friday afternoon in the middle of my mopefest, and we went out to the ramps to skateboard. I warned Luke to stay the hell away from me, and if he pulled my hair I'd cut his ears off worse than Vincent Van Gogh ever did. He didn't know what that meant but stayed away anyway. Sensing my pissiness, they all skated a good five feet away from me.

Jenny and Andrea and some friends of theirs were there swimming and hollering like wild banshees over at the pool. Chad twirled his whistle and laughed at Jenny as she did a half gainer, a forward flip, then two butt-busters. He would hold up his fingers with a score each time she surfaced from the water. She was a ham. I skated up and down the ramps, then hopped on the low-lying pipe and slid my board ten feet to the end. I ticktacked around and kept glancing back to see if Jenny and Andrea noticed I was there. I couldn't tell, but I kept looking to see if they saw me. I wanted them to.

Victor came out on the back stoop to watch us skateboard and read his paper and drink his beer. He smoked a cigarette and let it hang off of his lip when he turned the page. He read the sports page, mainly, and sometimes skimmed through the classifieds. Victor was on disability on account of his bad heart and bad back. He'd worked construction most of his life, but when he went on disability, he kept to fishing and drinking, his better occupations.

One of the girls with Andrea and Jenny had a guitar and she began singing some songs. Liking the way it sounded, I skated closer and listened. I watched her hands move up and down the neck of the guitar. Soft words floated on the humid air. It was a song about an angel flying from Montgomery. I listened to the lyrics and tried to cipher out where exactly Montgomery was. It sounded like a good place where dreams were "thunder" and lightning was "desire." I didn't understand that but it felt nice when it came out.

Andrea put her hands in the air, and said, "Sing it, Lucy! Sing it!" I thought for a second that they all looked like an Indian tribe. A heavier-set lady with dark hair strummed for the circle of friends around her.

Over and over again, she sang about how that angel flew from Montgomery. Maybe I could go there. The girl singing was pretty. I clenched the rungs of the chain-link fence and pressed my face against it. I thought about my job at the Curbside Café. Maybe I could waitress and then play the guitar there like how this lady was playing— maybe on Friday and Saturday nights.

All of a sudden, Jenny saw me from the ring of music and yelled my name.

"Looks like you got yourself a girlfriend," Luke said from behind me then skated back toward the ramp. He was far enough so I couldn't hit him but I balled my fist anyway.

"Shut up," I said under my breath.

For a moment, I acted like I didn't hear her and then she yelled my name again. *Holy shit.* I had to answer.

"Hey," I yelled, giving a wave. Victor ruffled his paper and drank from his beer.

Matt agreed with Luke, "Yeah, Piper. Looks like the girls are after you." He high-fived Luke and took his turn on the ramp. Traitors, all of them.

Bunch of Benedict Arnolds, I thought. I took off from the fence and went after Matt. I sailed right behind him, jamming my foot along the blacktop of the parking lot. I got side by side with him and then cut my board over on the back of his, purposely. Instead of wrecking him in my anger, I wrecked myself. I got up and shook off my own dumb damage. My skateboard floated drunk-like all the way to the curb by the edge of the pool. I shot up.

"Hey! Come over here, Piper." Andrea turned from her chair and held up her hand to cover her face from the sun. "Have you seen Someday?"

I shook my head and rolled my board over with one foot, fully embarrassed, cheeks on fire.

"Shit," Jenny said, "nothing at all. Has Victor called the pound?"

"Vera's been calling," Andrea interrupted.

"I think so. He called the Goochland pound," I squeaked out. I turned to look to see if the guys were watching. Chad, the lifeguard, was hanging by the edge of the pool listening to the concert. I looked at him and he winked at me. I averted my eyes.

The dark-haired girl stopped playing and put her guitar down gingerly on top of its case. "Oh, no," she said. "You lost your dog? Losing your dog sucks worse than anything in the world. I lost my dog one time and thought I'd die from trying to find her. Lucky for me, she was only three doors down in my neighbor's garage. They had accidentally locked her in. Boy, was she thirsty and hungry when we found her." She reached for her drink and swallowed long and hard.

"Piper, this is Lucy McGillicutty. Our famous singer, songwriter, nurse of all trades," Andrea said.

"Hi." I waved.

"Nice to meet you, Piper," Lucy said.

Jenny sat up and launched herself on her feet like a rocket. "Well, Jesus H. Christ. I am going to ask Victor myself what he's done. I've had about enough of this. Piper, you've been through enough. We need to find your dog. It may be hard—she might not come back. But we'll help."

"I thought you said that you would find her," I said impishly.

"Well, one way or another, we'll figure it out." Jenny looked at Andrea, who nodded.

Three of the other girls hanging in the circle of Indians all verbally agreed, too.

Pulling her shorts on, Lucy remarked that Jenny should take her biceps right on over there and show Victor who was boss. Everyone laughed. Jenny gave her the middle finger then pulled on some Adidas soccer shorts, squirmed into a tank, tromped through the gate of the pool area and then tromped all the way to our back porch. Instinctively, I followed.

"Victor?" Jenny put her hands on her hips.

"Yeah, whatcha need?" He continued to read without looking up.

"Victor, have you called the pound today to see if they might have Someday?"

"Uh-huh." He turned the page.

"Well?"

"Well, what? They don't have that lame old dog over there. Called twice already. Piper knows that. You don't need to be asking those questions when she already knows the answers."

"Did you go down there? Sometimes you have to go down there and look around because there are so many."

"I described to them that the dog had a funny paw. They looked. They didn't have any funny-lookin'-pawed dogs down there."

"She's not funny-looking," I said.

"Nobody asked you. Now go inside and get cleaned up. Get the stank off of you, you been hanging around over there at the pool."

"You know, Victor"—Jenny stepped forward—"I know guys like you . . ."

"You do. I didn't think girls like you knew any guys."

Jenny didn't stop. "Guys like you don't have any business raising a little girl like Piper because all you think about is your beer, your NASCAR and your stupid friends like that crazy-ass Clover. Where'd you find him? Huh? Need-a-slimy-dumbassfriend dot com? Oh no, that's too hard. Dot-coms are out, way out of your comfort zone."

"Problem with girls like you—" He turned the page. "The problem with girls like you"—he looked up at her—"is that you haven't ridden the horse hard enough to know the difference between an index finger and a cock that grows like a wet snake in the Garden of Eden. Now, don't tell me what's good and not good for me and my granddaughter here when you're busy buttering your girl's clam. Understand me? Or do you not know where good seafood comes from? Now get away from my porch before I bring out a clam cracker and bust up you and your pool party over there."

I was stunned. I'd never heard talk like that before. Clams? Index fingers? Cocks in the Garden of Eden? Religion was so confusing. I needed a cigarette to think that one out.

"You know, Victor. I'm not wasting my breath on you anymore. Help find her dog. That's the point, in case you lost it between your inchless dick and that cigarette you're holding."

"Get in the house, Piper. Now!"

• • •

He threw his paper in the boxwoods and kicked his beer. It splattered all over the sidewalk and broke the bottle in a gazillion pieces. Too many to count. Victor said the F word and gave her the double middle fingers. Worst I'd ever seen.

I flew up the porch steps and went into the kitchen

turned and watched from inside the screen door. Jenny walked away and gave him the middle finger back. Victor came in the house and after he took a long drink of Jack Daniels, he asked me to do the dishes. Moving quickly and not saying a word, I poured soap on them and began washing. He went upstairs, got his fishing gear and left. He said he'd be back in two hours. I knew what that meant. Six hours and a night on the couch.

Everyone was gone except the circle of women at the pool. I skulked around the apartment for five minutes to make sure Victor wouldn't come back for something, then I ran to the pool, hoping to hang out with them. For two hours, Lucy sang songs I'd never heard of and Chad and his girlfriend kept the pool open till the Wilsons told us to keep it down. Lucy had gotten really loud and funny and the whole neighborhood seemed to levitate when she was gabbing along. She asked if I knew any songs and I said that I liked what my dad used to like but couldn't remember what they were called. She smiled at me and then a girl named Alma went to the Coke machine and bought me one and I said, "Thanks."

It was the best I could do.

• • •

The next day was Saturday. Jenny had to work but Andrea promised me she'd take me to the animal shelter to see if Someday was there. I was right about Victor. He'd come in at two a.m and had passed out in his usual position on the couch with the clicker on his chest and the TV on, the volume up. So, it wasn't hard to give him the slip.

I met Andrea at the car and climbed in.

"You know, Piper," Andrea said, buckling up, "I have a friend who works at your school and I've been talking to him about you." She looked in the rearview mirror and pulled out. I looked into the side mirror to see my disheveled hair and my mass of freckles darkened from the sun. It was the first time all summer I had gotten away from the apartment complex and I looked—I looked like—nothing, I thought. "He would like to see you sometime and talk to you, if that's okay with you."

"I don't care." I shrugged. Meeting someone from my school sounded fishy. "Is he a teacher?" I asked after a minute.

"No, he's not a teacher," Andrea said. "He's a school psychologist and he's really cool. I think you'll like him. He's married and has a few kids that are there, too. First grade and second grade, I think." She turned at the light on Careybrook Road and we were on the main route to Richmond and the county shelter. "Do you know what a school psychologist does?"

"Not really. They talk to you and stuff and ask questions about your family?" I stared out the window.

"Yeah, that's right." She hesitated. "He's going to be up at school most of the summer and I thought I could ride you up to see him."

"I can walk."

"No, silly. I mean, I'll take you and introduce you. Maybe we can all go to lunch one day."

"At Curbside?"

"Do you like the Curbside Café?"

"Yeah. They have cool video games. Victor takes me there sometimes. It's where I'm going to work when I turn eighteen." Suddenly, I babbled out my plan about how I was going to have my own apartment and iPod and DVD and Someday, if we could find her, and maybe a big sectional couch like they show on TV. I'd live in the apartment complex next to ours and walk to work at the Curbside Café where I would ask people if they wanted ketchup with their fries and would they care for the check. It flew out of my mouth to Andrea "like monkeys out of my butt" as Jenny had described to me one day.

"Well, that's certainly a goal or two." Andrea must have thought I was nuts. I was sure of it. Now we had some school psychologist involved. Oh well, as long as he didn't give me a math test like Mrs. Svette's I would be all right.

For the rest of the ride, we remained silent. Andrea put in a CD of Melissa Etheridge and began to sing a song about chrome-plated hearts. She thumped her hands on the steering wheel like she was the drummer. I liked her, but I did not want to have anything mess up my plan. I didn't want to do any more damage like I'd done to Clover. Now Someday was gone and my mom's necklace was in the dirt. I needed to be more careful. I had a shiver. A shadow on my shoulder. I did not look.

Against all of my common sense that told me to be mad at God, I prayed anyway that Someday was there at the pound. I already had three holes in my heart from

Mom, Dad and Jack. Four holes in my heart was going to be too much if my dog wasn't there. I folded my hands in my lap and watched the brown and green county bend up and down—the car moved like a coasting glider over the hills and the natural curves of the heat-shimmering road. Staring at the corn and soybeans, I saw the old silos and barns and farmhouses wave out at me like they wanted to float away too, perhaps to a better place and time when it wasn't so hot and the ground was cool and the paint stayed lacquered and oily and tight on. Bales of hay dotted the barren wheat fields and looked too heavy to bear their own burden. When Andrea cracked the windows, I smelled the Virginia honeysuckle, the same honeysuckle I smelled every day at the pier, only this was stronger and I thought I might taste it if I stuck my tongue out. A sugar taste for sure, refined and not raw.

At one of the stoplights near the pound, I saw the 7-Eleven where my dad used to buy his cigarettes. I stared at it through the timing of the light, then looked at Andrea to see if she might have seen the same thing as me. My dad, mom and my brother sitting on the tailgate of the Ford Ranger, by the gas pump. Plain as day. They were not shadows today, not ghosts. Realer than that. I looked down at the fur I had pulled from my blanket and rubbed it between my fingers. When I looked up, my family was gone. I do not think Andrea saw what I saw. I did not speak.

When we got to the shelter, Andrea got out and told me to hold her hand. I did. She held it for a minute then explained to me that Someday might not be here and that

that was a pretty good possibility. My stomach dropped. I told her I understood.

Once inside the shelter, Andrea explained to the technician behind the counter all about Someday and what she looked like. The technician looked confused and asked three times about the bad paw. I stared at her. She was big and black as night. Her lips were thick and her nose was flat and her eyelashes were humongous. Her white coat had black and brown paw prints all over it, and she was smacking gum like nobody's business. She talked funny.

"I dunno. Some guy from down da screet said dat dog hed bit someone, I thinh. My jones takin' da dog down to lockup cuz some guy, I dunno, got fitty stitches or somfin."

"Who got fifty stitches?" Andrea asked.

"De ol' guy said dat da funky-pawed dog bit his friend and de dog had to go cuz he bit de guy bad. Said he had to go away to get rehabbed cuz his eye was bad, his leg was bad, and he sprained everything but his ass. Uh, sorry, little girl." She covered her mouth. "Dis is my firs week. So mebbe I'm wrong. Happened befo, you know. Das why I'm community service jones now."

I looked up at Andrea, who looked stunned by what the lady was saying to her.

"What exactly is lockup?" Andrea asked.

"Das where de dogs go 'fo dey go to the big hou upstairs, you know. Dogs dat have been in trouble wif da law. Dat's da closing room." The phone rang and she answered, "Counny poun, Shaneefa peekin.'" She smiled at me with her two front gold teeth. "I dunno if we got yo dog here—describe him again. What? Hole on. I'll look." She put the person on hold and looked at the two of us. "Now, whatcha all need now?"

"Well, we need to get that funky-pawed dog out for this little girl. It's her dog and I'm not sure why the dog is in lockup. Who brought the dog in? What's your name again?" Andrea asked.

"Shaneefa. Shaneefa Vernetta Daqwan. What's yose?"

"This is Piper. She owns the dog. I'm Andrea. I'm Andrea Cliff, her mother."

She lied right through her mouth.

"Who brought the dog in, Shaneefa?"

Shaneefa went back to the person on hold and told them to hold again. "Yo, Mr. Kistler. Yo, Mr. K., can ya pih up line two. Some bubba's blubbering ovah his loss dog. Ev'body's got some loss dog. Wearin' my black ass out. Oh, sorry, Piper."

"That's okay," I said.

Shaneefa shuffled through some papers and pulled out a file and opened it. She scanned the papers. "Loo like some dude named Victor Cliff brought dis dog in a few day back claiming dat da dog bit his friend, Clover Barry, and dat da dog had to be put down cuz it was da law."

There it was. Victor. My own grandfather had put my dog in lockup.

"Is Someday still alive? Is my dog still alive?" I could barely get out the words.

Shaneefa slowly peeked at me from behind the file. "Someday yo dog?"

"Yes."

Andrea put her hand on my head. "Someday's our dog. That's my crazy husband. He hates the dog and is always making stories up about how he's been bit, I've been bit, she's been bit, the postal carrier's been bit. We've all been bit. But the fact is, it isn't true. Someday—"

"Das a funny name for a funky-pawed dog. Ya name her?" She was looking at me.

"No," I said. "My mom did."

Shaneefa looked at Andrea then looked back at me. "Well, I ain't sho 'bout all dis. I probaly needs to ax someone since it's my firs week and all wif my service. Why dey put a big black-boned woman like me in here wif a bunch a dogs is pure madness. I'd ruther be's in jail watching TV wif my homies."

Andrea pulled out her wallet and pulled out three twenty-dollar bills. I counted them as she flapped them one by one on the counter. "Look, what Mr. Kistler back there doesn't know is okay by me." She handed Shaneefa the money.

"Oh, well," Shaneefa said. "Dis community service turnin' out to be right productive, I might say." She looked both ways and put the money in her pocket. "Come wif me."

She led us down a pungent hallway that smelled a mixture of urine, dog hair and Clorox. We went into another room where there were cages of dogs stacked on top of one another. Some dogs were sleeping, others were barking, and some were just staring. Shaneefa looked at her paperwork and was trying to match up something.

Andrea looked over her shoulder and helped. "She's in cage number forty-six." She put her finger down on the paper. "Forty-six, Piper."

"Foty-six. Das right, lil girl. Go on." Shaneefa pointed.

My heart pounded. We were at cage sixteen. *Forty-six minus sixteen. Forty-six minus sixteen.* I walked side-by-side with Andrea and Shaneefa till I couldn't stand it anymore. "Thirty!" I yelled. I started to run and yell her name. I ran and yelled. I yelled and ran. *Someday. Someday, Mom had said.* I counted the numbers as they flashed by. Thirty-eight, thirty-nine, forty, forty-one—

Forty-one was empty. Forty-two's nameplate on the side of the cage read, Bandit. Forty-three. I stopped looking at the dogs. I slipped at forty-four and landed flat on my face in front of forty-five.

"Safe," Shaneefa said. "You go, girl."

And there she was. My dog. I was on her level, my cheek pressed against the cement floor. I was looking at her, and she was looking at me. Her tail barely wagged and her eyes were the saddest I'd ever seen, dull and listless.

"Hey, Someday," I said. She whined and stayed down. "Hey, girl. I've missed you. Where have you been, Someday? I've been looking all over. Now look at where we've found you. You're right here. You're right here with me, girl. Oh, Someday, come here, girl. It's all right, girl. We're here now." I put my fingers through the grill of the cage. "You're my good girl."

"Sho do know what dat feels like," Shaneefa said. "Wantin' somein' and den can't gettin' to it. Hmm hmm

hmm. Sucks. Jail ih dah sorriest place ta be." She smiled with her gold teeth. "Dare's yo dog, little girl. Dare she is. Boy, she is a funky-pawed dog."

Andrea came from behind me. "Let's get this unlocked. What do you say, Shaneefa?"

"Lemme get Mr. Kistler. Dey don allow me no keys jus' yet. If ya know wha I mean." She smiled her gold smile wide and loud and handed Andrea Someday's file. She did a wink and Andrea nodded.

Andrea knelt down with me and we put our hands and fingers through the grill to pet Someday. Someday closed her eyes as we scratched her behind her dark rabbit ears and petted her soft short brown coat and the whiskers on her dark chocolate nose. Her fur was sticky and matted in places. I caressed her deformed paw. She raised it up in the air, and I pressed into the pads underneath and held onto it, like I'd never held onto anything in the whole world. Andrea and me knelt there together for a good while and stroked her. I told Someday that she was all right. "You're all right, girl. Everything's gonna be all right." Kneeling there with Andrea, it felt like the best church I had ever been to.

When Mr. Kistler got there, he asked for the file to double-check the particulars on Someday's jail sentence. Andrea had put the file in her bag. Shaneefa said she had already looked at the file, the dog had been misidentified, like in a bad lineup, she explained, and we could take her home.

"Well . . ." He paused. "Are you sure?"

"My husband is, well—" Andrea smiled at Mr. Kistler.

"He's a little befuddled in the noodle, if you know what I mean. This isn't the first time he's tried to get rid of her. Just look at her. How can a dog like that chase after someone and bite him. She can barely walk."

Mr. Kistler looked at Someday, her paw that was still resting in my hand through the cage.

"Well, all right, but I'm going to have to make a call—"

"Mistah K. You ain't got to make no call. Now I's already tole you dat dis dog is okay to go. Now, I knows I'm on community service an all, but de dog is good to go. Hear?"

"All right." He reluctantly opened the cage.

Someday could barely get up and crawl to the edge. Her eyes looked drawn and her nose was hot and dry. She whined. My hands shook. *Here she was. Here she was.* "Someday, shh-shh-shh. Good girl. You are my good girl." I looked to Andrea, who handed me Precious Pink's jeweled leash. I clipped it to Someday's tagless collar. I talked into her rabbit ears and kissed her. "Sweet dog. Sweet Someday. It's all right."

It was then that I noticed her low water bowl and uneaten food and the dried stains of vomit.

I steadied my hands. "Come on, girl." I helped my dog walk up and out of the cage then down through the hallway of barking dogs, a room full of assorted cats and empty cages. I looked at all of them. Their vacant, dark eyes all longing for something that I did not yet understand. My mind wanted to count again, wanted to count the cages and the faces. But all I could do was help my dog amble through what had been her prison.

I glanced back at Shaneefa Vernetta Daquan. She put her finger to her mouth to tell me to keep it all a secret. I nodded okay and then smiled at her. She smiled gappy and gold right back.

Once outside and into the car, Someday and I got into the backseat. Andrea was quiet till we got out on the street.

"Hallelujah! Amen! We got her, Pipe. We got her!"

She looked into the rearview mirror and I caught her eye. She looked back at the both of us for a split second. Our eyes smiled at each other and I put my arms and whole body around the love of my life—Someday Cliff. My dog, Someday. I closed my eyes and kissed her eyes, ears and nose. She licked me on my face and I giggled. I was secure in the backseat of Andrea's car with my dog. I wished that we could drive away somewhere far, perhaps Montgomery where the angel Lucy had sung about lived, a place where I could have my dog and Andrea and Jenny and even the cat.

Today, my heart would not get its fourth hole in it.

And, for a minute, with Someday and me in the backseat of Andrea's car, the three holes I had didn't seem so bad.

Chapter 9

"Did you ever read the story of Anne Frank?" Andrea asked as we motored closer to our apartment complex.

I thought for a minute. "No. I don't think so."

"Well, it's a story of a young girl and how she and her family had to hide away from the Germans during World War Two." She seemed serious. "It was very hard and they had to keep absolutely quiet for a very, very long time."

"We've read *The Red Pony* and—"

"Piper, we're going to have to hide Someday away from Victor. Anne Frank hid for a very long time so that the Germans wouldn't find her. We're going to have to act like Someday is Anne and that Victor is the German. And you are going to have to be the go-between. Understand. We just have to hide her till we figure out what to do."

"Did Anne Frank keep away from the Germans?" I asked.

"For a while she did. For a while."

"What happened to her?"

"What are you reading now?" She diverted me away from the question.

"Umm. Just some magazines and stuff I have at my fort," I responded and kissed Someday in between her eyes.

"Books, I mean."

"I have the mockingbird book, but I haven't read it. My teacher gave it to me because I got the highest scores on all of our reading and writing tests. She said I was two grades, at least, ahead of myself. Victor told me that she was lying when she said that, though and that I wasn't really that smart."

"Really? Mockingbird book? What's that? Oh, do you mean *To Kill a Mockingbird*?"

"I think that's the name of it." I scratched Someday underneath her collar. She was a tired dog who could barely keep her head up to look out the window.

"Wow, that's a good one. You should read—Oh, crap. Get down, Piper. Slide down in the seat. Victor is out by the maple tree picking up Someday's bowls. Get down." She looked at me in a panic in the rearview mirror and flailed her arm up and down like she was slapping flies against her seat. I jumped on the floorboard of the backseat. The German was outside drinking his American beer.

Someday, who evidently was now going to be Anne Frank, licked my face as I nestled in her fur beside her.

Andrea pulled in around front and told me to go home and act like I'd been out skateboarding. I did. She pulled out and left again with my dog.

Three hours later, Jenny came home in her mail truck from her Saturday delivery. I had been watching for her truck from my window. I had longed for a cigarette but waited in my room reading some short story about a young Russian girl skating at an ice rink and falling for some boy. Yuck.

I ran out to greet her and noticed that Someday was sitting up, funky paw and all, strapped in with an orange belt buckle in a small seat just behind Jenny's front seat. How she had gotten from Andrea to Jenny, I didn't know. When Someday saw me, she lunged at the belt to get out, straining. Her eyes looked swollen and tired and extra pink around the edges.

Jenny laughed. "Hold on, girl. I'll get you out. I know you want to see your mama."

She undid the belt buckle and Someday slid down onto the front steps of the mail truck. I kissed her and she licked my face clean.

"Hey, girl." Jenny ruffled my hair and hugged me. "I got your dog here. She's the best postal dog in the whole town of Goochland, Virginia. I tell you. She's a smart dog. You tell her to do something two or three times and she does it. I told her to sit and she did. I told her to stay and she did. And when I told her to eat a dog biscuit, it only took her once and she got it!" She rubbed the top of my head. I grabbed her hand. She held it for a second, squeezed it, then let go. I laughed at her silliness.

"What if Victor sees her?" I asked.

"It's okay." She looked around the cul-de-sac and then to the row of apartments. "He's not going to see her. Where's the last place you pegged he was?"

"In the kitchen reading the paper and drinking a beer."

"All right, go run up to the front window and then give me the high sign when he's not looking. Okay?"

I ran like a tear up to the double windows and peeked in. Still in the kitchen. I waved her on.

Jenny and Someday trotted to their front door. Someday stopped in her tracks and seemed to heave, then she blinked her dark eyes and glanced at me, almost like she was taking my picture. Sensing Someday's weakness, Jenny lifted her up in her strong arms, much like she'd done for me a few days earlier. Then Someday laid her head softly against her chest and shoulders. Jenny's shoulders were like iron and her arms and hands cupped my dog's tired body.

Something wasn't right. I practically leapt all the way down to their place. Once inside, I found that Someday was not her usual self. She had eaten two dog biscuits but had no interest in the wet food we put down for her. Andrea made boiled chicken and rice and Someday turned her nose up to that, too. We tried ice cream, Slim Jims, Goldfish crackers and Nilla wafers. She was listless, like half her life had drained out of her. She threw up three times before nightfall, and I kept telling Andrea and

Jenny I was sorry.

Jenny said, "Oh, shut the hell up and hand me a towel."

She elbowed me and then they both helped me clean it up. After the third time, Jenny finally called her vet, who told her what to do. We had to get the dog some medicine, but he wanted to check her out first. It was getting late but he said he would give her a look.

I rode with Jenny to the man's office, and he gave us medicine and a list of things to do. He was concerned, he said, slightly dubious about Someday and how she had gotten that sick and all, but in the end, he was hopeful she'd be all right. My words exactly. I smiled at him for helping. He waved us along and when Jenny drove by the same 7-Eleven I'd seen earlier in the day with Andrea, I looked away. We passed by the same farmhouses, the same silos. This time the darkening horizon shrouded them like a cloak; the edges of the fields buzzed with an aura that was not angelic, rather more stately and serene.

I held my dog close to me as the misty incandescence of the day turned to a starless pitch-black night till we got home.

Someday laid underneath Andrea and Jenny's round kitchen table for three days. It took three days for the poison to get out of her system, Andrea said. Someone had poisoned her, either at the pound or right before bringing her there. I got really mad and had another conversation with the Giver and Taker up in the sky. Then I did what I thought I should do—I stayed away from Precious Pink. I didn't want to rub any of my bad juju on her. I wanted desperately to have my dog back the way she was.

I laid underneath the table with her and, every now and then, I would swirl my fingers in her water bowl and then let her lick the water off. She accepted it when I did it that way. That was the only way she drank. Then, after a bit, I put small pieces of chicken in the palm of my hand, and she liked that, too. Mainly, though, I just laid on the floor with her, my arm around her, whispering in her ear that I loved her and that I didn't want her to go away ever again. "I need you, Someday," I whispered to her, looking in her eyes. I rubbed her belly and, most nights, Jenny and Andrea put a blanket on me and let me be. I ate two boxes of Goldfish crackers and never counted one.

Like a miracle, Someday got better. By midweek, she was up and getting along again. Jenny and Andrea and me laid out our plan to hide "the Anne Frank dog"—as we called her—in an apartment three doors down from the man who'd taken her to the pound and wanted her dead: Victor.

My luck began to change.

For the rest of the summer, I played the covert spy for Jenny and Someday. She took her on her postal route every day, and every day I greeted them at four thirty p.m. to get Anne Frank home, where I spent every evening with them. I didn't understand why Andrea and Jenny were doing what they were doing. We never discussed it. But every now and again, they'd be upstairs and I'd hear something about Victor and then something about my family and how horrible it all was. They never spoke to me much about it. I just went along like we were characters in our own book of twists and turns.

On most evenings, Andrea and Jenny and me walked Someday down by the creek and out to the river where we would skip rocks like my mom and me used to do. On the nights that Victor went to the Curbside to drink and play pool, I stuffed my bed with pillows like I'd seen in old movies, just in case he checked on me, and then spent the night with Andrea and Jenny. They made a small bed in their other bedroom and bought Someday two dog beds—one for downstairs and one for upstairs. Mostly, she slept with me. But when we were downstairs, she slept next to Precious Pink, who had a small cat bed next to hers. Andrea was nervous about Someday and Pink at first, but then she saw that Someday was no problem at all because of her limp and all and how pitiful her rabbit ears were when they laid flat against her head. Well, she realized that Someday and the Pink were an okay pair.

Jenny showed me how to teach Someday tricks. It was hard, but after a while Someday knew—sit, down, stay, speak, up like a prairie dog, roll over. Andrea's favorite: "Pick a Tarot Card." Jenny would shuffle the cards then spread them out on the floor. Someday, on command, would be asked to pick a card, and she'd sniff the whole deck up and down, put her bad paw on the one she wanted and pull it toward her. It was the hardest trick

Jenny had ever taught, but she said she liked it the best. Andrea read cards at the Fish Bowl Bookstore near where she was going to graduate school to become a licensed clinical something. I could never remember the last part. Jenny mentioned one day that she should take Someday to the store and have her fill in when Jenny went to lunch.

For three weeks, Andrea and Jenny planned a going-away party for their friend Vera, who was moving to Canada. They said she was fed up with the whole state of Virginia and how the bill for religious freedom—I think that's what she said—had been compromised by a bunch of Bush idiots. I knew he was the President, but I didn't know what they were talking about and what the fuss was about.

On the day of the party, I helped Andrea and Jenny decorate. We hung up all kinds of signs. There were rainbow balloons and rainbow banners, and Jenny made some homemade ones that said, "Get the hell out of Virginia, Vera. We can't handle you anyway." It was supposed to be funny and Jenny said that Vera would get it because she was smart. We had avocado dip, chip dip, shrimp dip, onion dip, till Andrea said this was no Forest Gump movie and Jenny said, "Come on, bubba. Be nice." She put her arms around her and kissed her in front of me while I pretended to hang a balloon on the wall.

I watched how they looked at each other and then how Jenny kissed Andrea's bottom lip real soft then paused for a second and kissed her upper lip. Andrea stayed still, perhaps a trick Jenny had taught her, and kept her eyes closed. Then really slowly, Jenny tilted her head and put her whole mouth on Andrea's like she was going to blow air into her. When Jenny pulled away, Andrea still had her eyes shut. When she opened them, they both smiled at each other, then glanced at me. I looked away quickly and didn't say anything.

"Piper," Jenny said, "I love this girl. You know that, right? You know what we are, right?"

I wasn't sure what she was asking me but said, "Yeah, you are my best friends. And Someday and Pink are your friends, too."

Andrea walked to me and put her arms around me and hugged me. "And we love you, Piper." Jenny hugged me, too, and said that group hugs were the best.

They were all right with me.

The party guests arrived shortly thereafter. There was Simon from the post office who worked with Jenny. The three girls I remembered from the pool came in with two twelve-packs of beer. Some guy named Brock Goldberg, who looked like a movie star, who brought Vera, the woman they were having the party for. Other guests arrived—a lady named Alma who taught school in the city. She had thick glasses and a small nose. Then this glammy glitzy lady arrived and beneath the makeup, I recognized Lucy McGillicutty, the crazy guitar-playing lady from the pool who had lost her dog once, too. They all had one thing in common. They were really loud. I sat and ate chips in the corner and watched the evening go from hugs and gentle kisses to "Right on, sister," and

"What in the world is going on?" "Freak out, no way!" was met with "Hey, get me another beer." It became a high-pitched phenomenon that I was not used to.

"How come all of the most serious lofty words in the world only have one syllable?" Vera asked while she sipped on a margarita. She had short-cropped hair and a wide Slavic face.

"What do you mean?" Alma asked her. Alma looked like Jodie Foster, my favorite movie star.

"Well, you know, I was thinking the other day about syllabification—"

"Oh, here we go," Lucy interrupted her. "Vera is going to pontificate like she's read the *Tao of Pooh* backward and she heard Beatles' music saying that Satan and Jesus are both dead so everyone just needs to buy a white T-shirt and go to the beach—"

"*Beach* is one," Vera said. "See, one syllable."

Brock came in from the kitchen and sat down next to Vera who was sitting directly across from me. "*Bitch* is another. See?" he mocked. "One syllable."

Alma leaned back and said, "Why is monosyllabic multisyllabic?" Everyone stared at her.

"Really," Vera went on, "if you think about it, it's true. Here, I'll give you a couple of examples: *God, love, hate, peace, dog, cat*—" She looked at Someday and Pink and pointed. "But it's really the big ones that I'm talking about, like *God, hate, love*—"

"*Male*," Brock interrupted and pointed to himself.

"Shut up, Brock," Vera said.

He laughed. "*Brock, shut, up*." He counted on his

fingers one, two, three. I immediately liked him and laughed.

Jenny said, "*Fear, truck, strength.*"

"Truck?" Andrea said. "Why truck?"

Jenny shrugged. "*Truck* is a good one."

"Fu—" Brock stopped as Andrea clamped her hand on his mouth. "Stop, I was going to say fudge. Trucks and fudge are good. Together. *Truck. Fudge.*"

One of the girls from the pool said, "How about *sex, drugs, rock, roll?*" Her friend slapped her hand.

Another one said, "Wait, wait. I've got a few. *Cheat, smoke, drink, ass, prick, chick, smile—*"

"*Laugh,*" Vera said.

"*Dick,*" Brock said. Andrea looked at him funny. "What? Dick's a good friend of mine."

"*Friend,*" Lucy said, "or better yet, *friends.*" Everyone drank to that one. I reached for my Coke and mimicked them.

"*Fear, yeah, yes, fire, earth, wind, stop, end, tree, breathe, air, soul, grass, pot, spank.*" Alma internally congratulated herself, it seemed, and pushed her glasses up on her nose.

"Oh, my, God." Lucy looked at her. "*We, have, a, weird, o.*"

"Piper." Vera looked at me. "Do you have one?" All eyes were on me.

I paused, thinking for a second. "No," I said.

She crinkled up her Slavic-looking, pockmarked face and smiled her gappy smile at me. "Piper, I believe you are the smartest one here. *No* is the best one I've heard yet."

She had saved me and we both knew it. I smiled back at her and took a sip of my Coke. Someday lay in the corner of the room on her bed next to a very pregnant cat. For a moment, I did not feel like the weight of the world was on my shoulders. I had shrugged like Atlas in the myth. Atlas shrugged. The heady shadows that lurked in and around me lifted, swirled up like feathers and danced away—my insides felt still. Vera had said I was smart.

"Speaking of Earth, Wind and Fire," Brock said, "let's play some music—"

Jenny turned the music on and I started up the stairs to fetch Andrea's Tarot cards. She had whispered in my ear to go and get them. "They are on the bedside table," she said. "Thanks."

I overheard Vera say that I seemed like a good kid. Jenny and Andrea mumbled about my parents and Victor and everyone seemed to go quiet. Listening for just a moment, I then sauntered up the steps.

Rarely did I go into Andrea and Jenny's room by myself. I crept in as if I were in some kind of sanctuary like in church. On the table there was a half-drunk bottle of water, a picture of Andrea and Jenny on some vacation somewhere, a pack of beat-up Tarot cards and a Bible. Sticking out from inside the Bible was a piece of folded paper. My nosiness got the best of me and I sat down to open it and see. It was a poem. The title was "Letter to Jenny's Feet." I laughed out loud at the title then read what I was sure I was not supposed to.

Letter to Jenny's Feet

My feet are the tips of matchsticks;
Illumined by the rubbing of yours and mine together.
The tendrils of toes, the arches of feet, the knot of
ankles.
My feet move like the flight of butterfly wings
Cupped to the echo of yours—closed, chrysalis.

Beneath the drape of sheets, the skin on skin strikes
and catching the flick of night sparks,
the news travels
through warm blood and spread of folded legs,
from the jointed couple moving—
rhythm still rhythm—rhythm still rhythm
a kindling of sulphuric flame.

Then, between my hips and among my own
Undergrowth, a pool of soul oil leaks,
Leaks from the throb of folded, soft wet pink.
Making beads of sweat like shapes of hearts.
Coin phrases between my thighs . . .
the cells of their own cocoon unable to breathe
or to speak
through the cipher of their own mashed syntax . . .
through warm blood and spread of folded legs,
from the jointed couple moving—
rhythm still rhythm—rhythm still rhythm.

Love, Andrea

• • •

I glanced at where it was in the Bible. It was in the book of Luke (I couldn't believe there was a book called Luke—yuck), where the most important commandment was starred. I quickly shoved the poem back into the Bible and ran downstairs to where everyone was sitting around the dining room table. Handing Andrea the cards, I resumed my position under the window with my Coke in hand. In my head, I silently counted the people at the party and was up to a good number till Vera interrupted my thought.

"So, Pipe. You mind if I call you Pipe?"

"No, ma'am," I said.

"Oh, please. Call me Vera. Or this crazy gal, Lucy here, sometimes she calls me Veer. I get off track sometimes, she says. So, anyway, Pipe, you live with your grandfather, I hear. What's his name?"

"Victor." I stared into my Coke.

"You and Victor get along pretty good since your parents died? By the way, I'm so sorry you lost them and your brother—"

"Pretty good," I answered. "He orders pizza sometimes, and after church on Sundays he picks me up and we go to the Curbside where the girl makes me a grilled cheese sandwich with brown sugar. Sometimes we fish. Most times not." I longed for a smoke and to go to my fort.

"Brown sugar—" Brock put his hand on his lips.

"Shut up, Brock. Let her finish," Lucy snapped.

"Does he go to church with you?" Alma inquired.

"No, he drops me off and then comes back to get me."

"Does he get you on time or do you have to wait?" Andrea asked then looked at Vera.

"Most times, I shoot baskets on the church rec yard for a while, and then he comes and gets me. I don't mind though." I wasn't sure why they were suddenly asking me all kinds of questions about Victor. I had already told the school psychologist that Andrea had taken me to a week earlier everything about Victor and my family. They must just be interested in me for me, I thought. Someday limped over and curled up next to me. I stroked her ears.

Out of nowhere, I felt Clover's presence at the window right behind me. The hair on my neck stood up and I looked at Precious Pink, who was licking her paw. A cold shiver went up my spine. Numbness settled along my skin. My stomach felt jiggy. My fort came to mind, where recently rain had swelled the edges of my magazines and book. The flag with the maple leaf on it was back on the ground and the red ink had bled all over the place.

"Well, Ms. Piper, if you are ever in Canada, please come and see me in my new chateau. I'm off after this party to live in the prettiest place in the world—Banff, Canada."

"Why are you leaving to live there?" I asked.

" 'Cause she's a pussy," Brock said.

"Watch your damn mouth, Brock," Jenny said.

"Jenny—" Andrea looked at her, surprised.

Under her breath Alma said, *"Damn, mouth, Brock, fame, hope, soul, war, hand."*

"I was thinking about the big abstract ideas, Alma, not anything concrete," Vera said.

"She's leaving because her mother died and left her a boatload of money and she hates Virginia for its big chasm between the right and the left. Right, Veer?" Lucy said as she shuffled Andrea's cards.

"*Chasm*." Alma put her finger up.

"*Or-chasm*." Brock changed the music.

"Jesus, I don't know why all of you fools aren't leaving. I'm not sticking around to see how the constitution of our state might or might not be amended." Vera gulped the remnants of her beer and went on. "We are in the twenty-first century and we are spitting on Thomas Jefferson's grave. I'm surprised Monticello hasn't just imploded from the crap those people—who are they? Marshall and Newman, the moral majority—have spread around. Only a marriage between a man and a woman will be recognized by this great commonwealth. And to top it off, they're saying that you can't create or recognize a legal status for unmarried straight people, too. They are bashing the gays and unmarried straight people who don't probably even give a rat's ass about marriage anyhow. Sorry, Piper." Vera took a breath. I shrugged. "You can't have a common-law marriage, property rights, legal contracts, hospital visitation or child custody. Businesses can be sued just for offering domestic partnership benefits. Talk about burning down the love institution. These family foundation people don't know that passing this amendment will actually affect the lives of millions of Virginians."

A girl who was dancing with another girl stopped and said to Vera, "Can you give me an example?"

"If Goldie Hawn and Kurt Russell moved to Virginia. You know they've been unmarried and together for a bunch of years. Let's say if they moved to Virginia and drew up a last will and testament saying that if one or the other dies then he or she—whoever is left living—gets the house, you know, custody of the dogs. But, but, but if this amendment passes and Goldie's brother comes along and says, 'Unh-unh, I want Goldie's house and all of her possessions because I'm her brother and the state of Virginia doesn't recognize them because they are unmarried.' Then, guess what, people? Guess what? The brother wins. The evil brother from Idaho wins. For example." She put her hands in the air. "Can you believe it?"

"Wow," the dancing girl said.

"Good one. Very monosyllabic," Vera said.

"Piper." Alma looked at me and then tried to explain. "Vera lost her girlfriend a few years ago to cancer. There was a situation with her being allowed to see her in the hospital and all. Very long story—"

"So, I'm going to Canada because you can be anything you want up there. It's too cold up there for them to worry about anything else but trying to keep warm. They keep their laws off people's minds, hearts and bodies," Vera said.

"*Mind, heart,*" Alma said.

"Alma, for Christ's sake, we're done with that one," Lucy said.

"Sorry." She smiled at me and I smiled back.

"Abstract, that's right, Alm." Vera looked at Lucy and rolled her eyes.

The party switched gears at that point because everyone seemed to be out of beer or a drink at the same time. After Andrea read Tarot cards and announced to everyone that "Mercury must be in retrograde," we all walked Someday down to the river.

It was dusk.

When we got close to the pier, Vera talked with me and asked me some more questions about Victor and all. She told me again how sorry she was about my parents and brother and then asked me how they died.

"In a car crash taking my brother to the hospital," I said. "He'd cut his hand and needed stitches."

"Where were you when it happened?" she asked. We walked by my fort. "Were you here at your fort?"

"No."

"Were you at school?"

"I don't know. I can't remember. I think I was home."

"You stayed at home while your mom and dad took your brother in the car?"

"In the truck—I think they were in the truck. I don't know."

"That's all right, sweetheart." Andrea came from behind. "You don't have to remember right now. Remember what the nice man at school said?"

"The psychologist?" I asked.

"Yes." Andrea handed Jenny her drink and took my hands and looked at me. "What did he tell you on your visit?" She squeezed my hands then let go.

"That I don't have to remember anything till I'm ready?" I responded and looked at Jenny.

"You're goddamned, right, Pipe. You don't have to remember anything till you're ready." Jenny rubbed the top of my head like she always did.

"When I'm Goddamned ready!" I said to Jenny.

"That's right." She kissed me on the cheek.

Lucy came up and the party caravan edged toward the rickety pier. "Okay," she said. "Anytime I hear the word psychologist, I know a party is getting boring. Everyone!" she exclaimed. "I want everyone to officially get out of your own heads, stop the monosyllabic insanity and let's get this party started. Vera, get your dancing shoes on."

"They're on, Lucy." Vera looked down.

"Oh, Jesus. Did you already forget what a euphemism is, you ol' dumb librarian? Alma, hand me my guitar." Everyone gathered around Lucy like when we were all at the pool that time. "I want to sing a song for Vera and her next journey into her goofy life." She swallowed hard on her beer and tuned her guitar.

Alma pushed her glasses up. "She's not goofy, Lucy."

"Alma, sorry for the confusion," Lucy went on, "you're the goofy one."

Lucy picked the chords to get the sound right in her ear. "I'm taking suggestions on a song. What do you all want to hear?"

Alma jumped up. "Oh, Lucy. Please play that song. Hmm. You know. 'I can see clearly now the rain is gone.' Play that one."

"Uh, no," Lucy responded. "That is the sappiest song of the twentieth century."

Brock said, "'Brick House.' One syllable each." Alma smacked him on the back of the head.

Lucy stopped. "I've got one. But I need my drunk backup singers." The three girls came in close. "Can you do the whoo-hoos?" Lucy asked.

They nodded. One said she could sing the bop-bops. I sat and listened.

Lucy said, "This one's for you Vera. You loser. We love you. I've changed the pronouns on this one to make it work. You know, Vera, Virginia has proved to be too much for you." She strummed the guitar. I wanted to play it, too. It was so cool.

"Whatever you say, Lucy." Vera smiled at her and Brock.

Lucy started to sing and everyone immediately knew the words and music. I wasn't aware of anything but the music issuing like flowers from Lucy's lips. I felt floaty inside. When she got to the chorus, everyone was doing the full version. It was "Midnight Train to Georgia" but instead of "he's leaving," it was "she's leaving."

When Lucy sang the last two lines about how she'd "rather live in her world" than "be without her in mine" of the last chorus, almost at once everyone started to cry. This woman, Vera, was leaving, I guess now on a train to Georgia, and everyone was upset. I asked Jenny why everyone was crying—even her.

Jenny whispered in my ear, "Vera is like the one person we've all looked up to and loved the most of anyone ever.

You know what I mean?"

I whispered in Jenny's ear, "Like I love you?"

"Yes, darlin', like you love me."

Lucy and the traveling party sang more songs late into the evening. Someday remained close to me and Jenny and Andrea. Every now and then I would glance to my right and then to my left to see the skirts of shadows. There were none. For the whole night, no shadows—good, bad or indifferent.

I didn't know it, but a new chapter in my life was just beginning.

Chapter 10

On some days throughout the summer, Jenny let me ride with her in the postal truck. That way, I could be with Someday and take her for a walk when Jenny was on break. I got to know more people and dogs in my neighborhood than I ever thought existed. She had 416 stops. I counted one day. Someday's rabbit ears sailed up and down in the wind and it was boiling hot in the truck, but I didn't care. Jenny kept the fan on high and the truck in gear practically the whole time. She played music and we sang along with all the windows wide open. She played Indigo Girls, Melissa Etheridge, Led Zeppelin, Melissa Ferrick, a dance mix from the Seventies that included "The Hustle." Whenever this one played she would get

out of the truck and dance to it, sometimes dragging me
with her. She taught me how important it was to take care
of Someday and make sure she had enough water and
treats and stuff like that. Jenny was really smart.

I watched her use her muscles and veiny hands to pull
mail from the trays on the left—how she had everything
matched up I could not understand—and then slap
them into the mailboxes through the door on the right,
then speed to the next stop. Sometimes it felt like I was
in an amusement park and I was on a ride. She would
zoom through cul-de-sacs and zoom down every tree-
lined street like her truck automatically knew the way.
I laughed at how she jerked to a stop then pulled away
quickly. Someday stuck her head out the window on the
opposite side and seemed to enjoy it too, especially the
long stretches on her route where she picked up speed.
Someday's ears flapped extra hard in the wind. I laughed.
Jenny gave me sunflower seeds to chew on and a spit can
to boot. A pack would last me two days and then she
would stop at Grant's convenient store to pick me up
some more. She chewed on mini-Bazookas (after reading
her fortune) and I ate the seeds. Jenny talked a little, but
mainly she sang and chewed her gum and hustled harder
than anyone I'd ever seen. Every day, at the end of her
route, she religiously played her favorite: "Fool in the
Rain" by Led Zeppelin. She said it was her mantra. I got
to know all the words and we sang it and played air guitar
together.

Stopping by my fort with Someday one Sunday
afternoon when Victor was gone, I noticed, once again,

the rain damage and the way I had left the place unkempt after my Fourth of July kick fest. Besides a few minutes at Vera's party, the last time I had spent any real time there was when I clobbered Clover. I tried not to think of him and his scruffy beard and beer breath coming down on me. He had been gone nearly five weeks. I crossed days off of my calendar and looked ahead to when Clover would be back—early September, I thought. I smoked a cigarette. It was stale but I smoked it anyway. I repositioned some plywood, restacked some magazines and read the dedication in the *Mockingbird* book. It said, "Lawyers, I suppose, were children once." I read it four times. Then I said it aloud, once.

I heard Matt and Luke and Buddy skateboardin' up on the hill. I had stayed away from them since I had been hanging around Andrea and Jenny.

Out of nowhere, this huge bug landed on my neck. It was a spricket, a cross between a cricket and a spider, and they scared the hell out of me. I grabbed at my neck and squished it between my fingers, then I got up and did the heebee-jeebee dance all around my fort. I kicked the magazines and yelled the worst word ever. *Fuck*. Andrea would not like that. Hesitating, I observed the leaves moving with the sticky wind.

I had heard my dad and mom yelling it more than once and Victor said it all the time. "Get the fuck out of here," he used to yell at Someday. Then one time after everyone had been killed, I was looking at Victor in the living room and he said, "What the fuck are you lookin' at?" I just shrugged and walked away.

Once, I counted how many beer cans were in the refrigerator. Thirty-six. I stole one and drank it with a smoke at my fort and threw up. I made a compact with myself then that smoking would be my vice, not drinking. Plus, every time he got drunk, he got to yelling and saying stuff and mumbling—none of it I could ever understand. Victor was a damn kraut. Hitler. A spricket with a German helmet stuck on his head.

I wiped the squishy remains of the spricket on the floorboard of my fort. Finishing my cigarette, I ground it out and then went to Andrea and Jenny's to get my skateboard. They had given me a key and I went right on in as usual.

This time, though, neither Andrea nor Jenny were in the kitchen or the living room. I called for them but figured they must be at the pool. Jenny was a diver.

Then I ran upstairs to my room to get my board, taking the steps two at a time like Jenny. At the top of the landing, I saw that their bedroom door was open. I approached with a sense of delicacy and when I peered around the doorway, I saw what I was not supposed to see. Right away, I knew for sure I wasn't supposed to be seeing what I was seeing. For a second, I was paralyzed as I stared—numb—my feet were glued to the floor. Jenny was lying on top of Andrea. Then Andrea grabbed the back of Jenny's hair and pulled her head down to hers and kissed her. Andrea's face was burnt red on her cheeks. Jenny was sweating, her curly strands of hair pressed against her temple as I had seen them when she was working. Their tongues were all over each other's neck and face and lips and nose and eyelids. How they were keeping up with each other, I didn't know. They went slow, then fast. The covers were all over the place. The comforter was on the floor and so was half of Jenny's postal uniform and some silky underwear. Andrea grabbed at the sheets and then Jenny got up on both elbows and put her hands on the sides of Andrea's face. She stroked and caressed Andrea's hair around her ear and then put her whole mouth right onto Andrea's lips. Andrea moaned. I had never seen anything like it—*holy cow*! Then Jenny was whispering something but I couldn't hear. I became bug-eyed and semi-catatonic.

They were doing it.

Grabbing my skateboard, I flew down the steps. I filled up Someday's water bowl and shot outside. I joined Matt and Luke and Buddy on the ramps till sundown. The whole time, I kept picturing what I had seen.

Then, when I thought a half of a millennium had passed, I headed back to Andrea and Jenny's apartment and the shadow ghost of my dad seemed to show up before me. I sat down on the curb near my basketball hoop. *Wait here with Someday, Piper. We'll be right back. Your brother needs stitches and needs to go to the hospital.* Then, my brother. He was looking at me through glazed eyes. He didn't say anything. Then my mom. *Piper, go upstairs and get a washcloth. Get it cold and we'll put it on his head. Dad and Jack had a time here with some fishing string. Go on. Go on.* I had done as she told me. Almost always, I did.

"Yo, little girl! Come on home and help me with this

TV set." It was Victor out on our porch.

I turned toward my apartment. I would have to slip away later, I thought.

"What you been doin'?" he asked.

"Boardin'," I answered. I had barely spoken to him since he'd tried to get my dog killed. Over a month of one word answers and nondescript replies.

Mr. and Mrs. Wilson glanced over at us as they got into their car. "Hey, Mr. and Mrs. Wilson." Victor smiled.

Mrs. Wilson did not wave but looked at me and they hurriedly got in the car. Mr. Wilson nodded and tipped his hat. That was it.

"You ain't been hanging 'round those dykes, have you?" Victor scratched his belly then burped.

I didn't respond but brushed passed him. I wasn't sure what a dyke was.

"Get me a beer, will ya? I don't want you hanging around those dykes because they may rub off on you, or worse, turn you gay. I don't want a gay granddaughter 'round here. My life's hard enough just keepin' food on the table and drawers on your ass to get you to school. Those lezzies are weird people and I don't want you over there. Are you listenin' to me?"

"Yes." I handed him his beer. "What's a dyke?"

"A dyke? Well—a dyke. Hmm. I'm not sure what a dyke is. I think a dyke is like a butch girl. They like to finger each other. Now, I know you're young, but that's what they do. They finger each other in between the legs because they don't like men and their penises. Don't you let them near you and try and do that. I know it sounds harsh. But you have to know this. They might try and pull the fast one on you and you need to be ready. It's in the Bible that it's a sin to finger someone of the same sex. I think it's in Genesis or Solomon or somewhere around there. Understand?"

I nodded. I guess that's what they had been doing earlier. Fingerin' each other. There were blankets over them so I wasn't sure about the finger part. I couldn't tell.

"The Bible says it's wrong?"

"Yep. Right there in everything big old Moses said." Victor turned the volume up on the TV. "They should be teaching you that sometime in Sunday school, I think."

"Why is it wrong?"

" 'Cause it just is and what the Bible says is the law of the land. Homos been screwing up everything for a long time. Now they got Oprah on their side and then Ellen's one of 'em. I heard on the news where the homos are blamed for just about every natural disaster we've had in the last few years—tsunami, nine-eleven, Katrina, Iraq." Victor counted them on his fingers. I didn't know who Sue Namy was but I'd heard of Katrina and 9/11 and had seen some stuff on Iraq. "Just stay away from them. They are helping to create catastrophes everywhere." He turned his face to the TV and that was that.

I went to my fort to think all of this over. Victor, the German spricket. Now, Andrea and Jenny were helping to ruin the world. I couldn't figure it out. I smoked three cigarettes and tried to understand. I reopened the mockingbird book and read the first page about a young girl and her brother in Alabama. I wondered if it was near Georgia, where I thought Vera was now headed. I closed it after the first page and looked to the sky through the arcs of the oak trees hovering over my fort. I stared for a long time and tried to think.

But when I started home to Andrea and Jenny's apartment, I was sure of one thing. My dog was with the world ruiners and that's the place I wanted to be. It may have been against everything in the Bible and the world. But my only world now consisted of them and my dog.

It was a pivotal moment for me. It was a pivotal time in my world.

I just didn't know it.

Chapter 11

My life got better till September hit and I had to take math again. My fear of fractions and measurement came up during the days prior, but I squashed them down by playing basketball. Jenny had taught me how to dribble and shoot from the baseline extended and from all around the chalky key we drew in the middle of the cul-de-sac. We played horse, pig and around-the-world. Jenny was awesome. She could swish it from over thirty feet away and never smiled or nothing. She would just do it over and over and over each time I passed the ball to her. When Andrea was studying for her tests for school, Jenny stayed extra long, sometimes playing long after the sun went down and the streetlight went on. And when Victor was at Curbside or out fishing, we would bring Someday out of hiding and she would hobble around the key and bark at us. When the ball banged off of the sewer, Someday would run after it and drool all over it. Jenny said that dog drool was good for shooting. I agreed. She taught Someday and me more tricks but the rides in her postal truck stopped when school started. I missed the music and the silence the hum of the truck brought to us.

Before school began, Andrea drove me to the Wal-Mart all the way into Richmond and she bought me a new backpack that had eight different compartments for putting things in, a nice ruler and some Goldfish crackers. Andrea told me that she was studying to work in a hospital environment like Lucy McGillicutty was. She was getting her master's degree. She complained about how she hated school, though, and that science and math were her hardest subjects. Listening to her made me feel better, like I wasn't the only one who had counting problems.

Even Someday had a new collar by the time Labor Day ended and I had to face Mrs. Svette and imagine her bulbous jaw muscles, metaphorically clenching down on me and the rest of the class. I put Someday's old collar in a special compartment in my backpack for good luck. Seventh grade was upon me.

So, the first day of school came down on me. Intently, I looked at Mrs. Svette and had made sure my pencils were sharpened and my paper was ready. With her lips pursed, she spoke about rules and the importance of math, in case any of us wanted to be engineers, scientists or physicists, in case any of us could conjure that up. The only thing that I could conjure was how I wanted to play for the girls' basketball team.

Carly Hasselbaum stuck her tongue out at me when she passed by the class's window. I stuck mine out at her and Mrs. Svette asked if I was paying attention. I said, "Yes, ma'am," and looked down.

After math and before lunch, I said hi to Mrs. Raymond, my favorite teacher from last year. She asked if I read any books over the summer and I told her I'd learned about Anne Frank and that next up was that mockingbird book she gave me. She said I really ought to read it. She didn't know that I had put Crazy Clover's eye out with it. I had kept that a hard secret. I didn't want that craziness screwing me up and my plan. I just wanted to make the basketball team, and then in five and a half years I could have my own place with my dog. Only five and a half years and I would have my own apartment with Someday and I could wait tables and eat at Curbside and play and sing like Lucy McGillicutty.

By the end of the first week, I had gotten through three math worksheets but Clover was back. Holy brain damage.

When I got home on the Friday of the first week, Victor was fuming mad and him and Clover were heavy into the beer. On the coffee table lay a letter from the school and child protective services.

Victor told me to sit down and said that we had a big damn problem. "Looks like those nasty dykes of yours are calling for the school and child protective services to send out a social worker on your behalf, Piper. Looks like those girls are wanting the cops to do a little evaluatin' 'cause they think I ain't good enough to take care of you. This letter"—he threw it at me—"this letter here says that there are signs of neglect and that I'm not fit to raise your sorry ass. Clover here says he seen you going over there some this week since he got back. Is that right? Have you been goin' over there? Answer me!"

"Yes."

"What for? I told you they was no good. I told you they was sick, bad people. Why did you go and disrespect your poor grandfather like that. What have I ever done to hurt you?" He seemed sad, desolate, melancholy almost.

I shrugged.

"Answer your grandfather, you little liar." Clover limped over my way. He grabbed my shirt sleeve and pulled my backpack up. His eye was puffy from scar tissue and was half-closed shut like he'd been punched in it. His breath could kill a squirrel.

I froze in my tracks.

"Leave her be, Clover," Victor said. "She don't know any better."

Clover ignored him. "You like hangin' 'round 'em, don't you?" He stank of beer. "What you doin' over there all the time? I'll tell you what they're doin', Vic. They got them voodoo Tarot cards out and they witchin' around like a bunch of crazy Indians. You see them touch each other? Huh? You see 'em kissing each other. Huh? You see 'em hold hands? They put their tongues in each other's mouths?" He stuck his tongue out and vibrated it in front of me.

"That's enough, Clover. I said let her be." Clover let go of me.

He was right. I had seen them. I stood there with my head down. Pictures and images of everything I'd seen Andrea and Jenny do came to my mind's eye. Lips. Kisses. Smiles. Hugs. Someday. Precious Pink. Vera and Lucy singing songs. Brock cussing like a sailor. Jenny cussing like a sailor. Blankets moving around their sweaty heads. It all whirled around in my head like flashing bulbs. My head buzzed. My eyes crossed. The air in my lungs compressed down into my stomach. The room spun around much like the stars had zinged around like a spin top the night I had gnashed Clover's eye and Someday had gone missing.

I ran two steps at a time up and into my room. Laying down on my bed I could hear Victor and Clover murmuring over what the letter said. I was sick to my stomach.

Then the shadows came, closer to my shoulders than ever, and Someday was three apartments down. I had nothing to hold onto but the sheets, and I shut my eyes so the shadows would go away.

Then in my ear the shadows talked to me.

Someday is sick, Piper. You stay with her till we get back from the hospital. My mom kissed me on the forehead, her Celtic cross dangling before me. The silver sparkled off the light from the window.

Suddenly, I saw it all like an illusion come real. My dad, mom and my brother, Jack all getting into Victor's truck, the fishing poles hanging over the tailgate. There'd been a sharp knife, blood, a bone showing—Jack's. My dad was holding onto Jack and Victor threw a beer can down and got in behind the wheel. Mom had come in for her purse. She had come in for her purse. I could see her. She had come in for her purse. And then, I was at the window. Someday was sick. I had to stay back. She had come in for her purse. The beer can laid in the grass by the truck. Dad held Jack. Jack was still and scared. He was so still. My brother was still. My mom did not look back my way.

I waited all night.

It took them thirty minutes to die. All three of them "on impact," the people said later at a funeral I barely remembered. I was almost eleven years old.

It took the police all that night, the night they died, to get to me—to find the sole survivor. They put me in the police car and drove me to my aunt's house—an aunt who never had much to do with me. Victor showed up with stitches in his head, got me and took me to the Curbside Café, where we didn't talk. He got so drunk that the waitress drove us back to his empty, lonely apartment. Someday was left behind at my parents' house. I forgot all about her.

Snap. That was how it all happened. I never went back to my house. I never got my stuff. Victor said it all got sold. Two years. Everything I owned and my family gone in the instant a car came sideways at the intersection of Gayton Road and Old Mill Road. Someday had held me back. For two years, I blamed it on her and how I had tormented those cats.

And now, the school and the law. I guessed they were going to try and put me somewhere—somewhere else. But I liked where I was. I had two homes—one with some of my stuff and one with Andrea and Jenny. Maybe Jenny and Andrea were wrong? Maybe Victor was right about them and the Bible. Who wrote the Bible, anyway? Who was this guy, Jesus, and why was he being so bossy? Maybe I was supposed to be somewhere else, but they were all I had. Maybe they wanted me somewhere I did not want to go. I was more confused than in Mrs. Svette's math class. I would have to consult my calendar and smoke four cigarettes to work through this one.

I didn't know anything for sure except that a social worker was coming the next week and we needed to get things squared away or Victor might be in trouble. I was still mad at him for taking Someday to the pound—very mad at him! But I figured that if they took me from him, then I would lose everything I had worked for in my head and my three-holed heart—Andrea and Jenny, for starters, but mainly my dog.

He made me scrub the stove and the baseboards as raw as I could get them. Next, he managed some laundry, but his hands shook when he folded it so he let me do it. He took me to Target and got me one new pair of jeans and two pink shirts and a new pair of shoes he thought a girl ought to wear. I cringed when I looked at them.

He got rid of most of the beer cans and told Clover to stay away from the apartment because he was afraid he'd scare the hell out of the social worker with his crazy eye and new limp. "Jesus, Clover, you look like a Captain Goddamned Crook. I'll meet you at Curbside when it's all over. Go scare the waitresses till the interview is over." It was practically the first time I had seen Victor do anything besides drink beer.

He appeared to be more worried than I'd ever seen him. Clover hovered around me some but did as Victor said. So I didn't see him much while we were trying to make the Norman Rockwell plates and the sign that said "Bless this House" come true in an apartment that was stuck in the tired town of Goochland, Virginia.

We held our collective breaths and waited.

In September, the social worker came by four times. The first three times, I had showered and slicked my hair down. The new stupid white sneakers made my heels hurt. Victor had on a white button-down shirt and khaki pants I had ironed, and we answered all the questions right. She asked things like what time I came home from school each day and then asked Victor if he was here. He said, "Most definitely. I'm always here to greet her." He lied, but I went along with it.

On her third visit, she asked me if she could see my room. I said, "Yes, of course." I said it like I was prim and proper. I showed her my bed and the window I looked out on the nights I wasn't over at Andrea and Jenny's. I didn't tell her the Andrea and Jenny part for fear she'd read the Bible. Pointing to the cul-de-sac, I told her I shot baskets there. She asked me how I got along with Victor. I said that we go on along pretty well most days.

"Most days?" she shot back.

"Every day," I corrected myself.

She saw pictures of my family and didn't say anything. I guessed she had heard. Victor and me both exhaled when she left after doing her white-glove test. After each time, Victor took me to Curbside and got drunk and fed me as many grilled cheese and brown sugar sandwiches I wanted.

The fourth visit was a surprise.

The social worker waited two solid weeks and then sprang on us like the Germans. It was six o'clock in the evening and Victor was passed out on the couch in his own pee. I was on my way to Andrea and Jenny's to take Someday to the river and then spend the night. The lady asked if she could come in, and then before I could say anything, she just did. There were Budweiser beer cans all over—four on the round table, three on the kitchen counter, one on top of the dryer, two atop the pizza box in the trash that hadn't been taken out in a week. The dishes in the sink were undone, dead soldiers. She took a piece of paper and a pencil out of her purse and began taking notes. I followed her around with a trashcan, picking up the empty cans and trying to kick laundry into the dusty corners. I tried to say it was all right but could not muster up the words.

To top it off, Crazy Clover knocked on the front door. Victor did not budge. Everything began to come undone.

The social worker lady opened it and then stepped back, stunned at the drunk Frankenstein in front of her. He explained that he was my uncle and came in. I just stared. Clover said that Victor had epileptic fits and that sometimes he wet himself. He told her not to be scared of his bad eye and all, that he'd had quite a fall on the Fourth of July. It seemed to assuage her momentarily.

I slipped out the backdoor and ran the three doors down to Andrea and Jenny's.

"Yo, Pipe, come here. I want you to see something," Jenny put her book down on the round table. I checked the title. Not the Bible. Phew. Andrea stirred a kettle of steamy stew on the stove. Andrea smiled from ear to ear. Why in the world were they so happy? My panic got worse.

"Go on, Piper. Jenny has a surprise for you. It's a glorious day," Andrea said. *Glorious. Glorious.* They did not know that my apartment was under siege. A social worker as a kraut—Crazy Clover in the fray—and Victor passed out. All just three doors down. I was marginally confused by Andrea's giddiness but happy to be, momentarily, away from the scene of the crime at my house.

"Follow me, but be very careful or I'll kick your ass."

"Jenny," I said. "I need to tell you—"

Jenny held her index finger to her mouth then rubbed my head. I shut up.

We tiptoed up the steps. In the bedroom where I always slept, Someday was sleeping curled up like a sack of sand. But Jenny gently pushed me to see that in the crook of her belly lay Precious Pink and three little newborn kittens, a white one, a black one and a marbled-looking one. Each one had paws that looked like they'd been dipped in speckled paint. All were asleep.

"Are the kittens okay?" I asked. "Is Pink okay?" I was worried and looked to Jenny.

She squatted down and hugged me.

"Everybody's okay, Piper. Including you."

Then, I got my freak on.

I cried. I let go and I cried. Someday was all right, the kittens were all right and me too. Jenny said that her and Andrea loved me. I had not heard the "love you" words said to me in a long while. I said that I loved her, too. After all—I sucked in hard—they'd been hiding my dog for nearly two and a half months and they'd made a spot for me with all the things I loved: a subscription to *Skateboardin'* magazine and three tank tops I had seen at Wal-Mart, and, just recently, Jenny had bought me an iPod where she had already loaded all the songs we had sung in her postal truck. I felt like this had to be heaven. *Heaven.* I longed for my mother and father and brother to see that I was here and that I was okay. Chills ran up and down me, pricklies all over as I smashed my face and my whole body into Jenny's. I sobbed and breathed and sucked air funny and then my face got fiery hot.

"I got you," Jenny said. "Shh, shh, shh, shh, pretty girl. I've got you. Somebody's got to have you. By damn, you've got the prettiest eyes I've ever seen."

"The lady's at my apartment," I said. I wiped my tears, then hugged Jenny again.

"What lady?" Jenny asked.

"The social worker from the county. Victor is passed out and Clover's there, too. It's all a mess. Something bad's going to happen. He might hurt her—"

"Well, honey. I've got to tell you something—" She stopped. "He might hurt who?"

"Clover might hurt—" I bit my tongue.

Jenny stared at me for what seemed like an eternity. "Clover. Clover. Did Clover ever hurt you, Pipe?"

I didn't say anything. I wasn't sure. He never smacked me around.

"Did he touch you funny, Piper? Is that what happened on the Fourth of July? Did he hurt you?"

I was mute. The kittens were right in front of me.

"Piper, I swear if he hurt you, I'm going to kill him. Now, tell me. Tell me the truth. Swear. Piper, swear."

"I swear," I said.

"What did he do?"

"He kinda held me down and tried to kiss me—" That's all I got out before Jenny was down the stairs two at a time. I screamed after her, "I don't want the kittens to die!"

I heard Jenny scream everything I had just said at Andrea and Andrea tried to calm her down.

"It's no use going over there," Andrea explained, "especially if a social worker is there." Apparently, if Jenny exploded with her hot temper, then it would hurt me. I could hear them arguing from the landing at the top of the stops.

Jenny said she didn't give a shit about the social worker and she was going over to have it out with all of them. She was sick of the bullshit. The neglectful sick son of a bitch had it coming and she was going to give it to him.

"What are you going to do?" Andrea asked. "Hit him

with a tray of mail? What about a large Express box, Jenny? That ought to really hurt. Here, take my pack of Tarot cards. That'll put the hurting on him."

Jenny slammed the door. I went downstairs and into the den. Andrea flew from the kitchen and came to me and hugged me. I said again that I didn't want the kittens to die.

Andrea assured me they wouldn't, but I wasn't too sure. She went into the kitchen and got me a cold Coke and some water for herself. She began talking to me and then Someday came down the steps and limped toward me. I reached down and patted her on the head and rubbed her rabbit ears.

Just when I thought it couldn't get worse, it did.

Evidently Clover had left the scene of the first crime and decided to come a few doors down to create the second crime. He opened the front door to Andrea and Jenny's apartment and stood there with his hands on his hips.

"Whoa, there. Just what do you think you're doing, mister?" Andrea moved to the middle of the room in front of me.

"I've come here to get her." He pointed to me. Someday growled and walked toward him. "Shut up. You stupid lame-ass dog. That dog of yours got quite a bite, little girl." He looked at me. "I thought I'd seen you with her down at the river by the pier recently with your girlfriends. That dog shoulda been put down two months ago. Even Victor agreed. See here, little Ms. Jiggily Wiggily, when we's all worried about you that night, long comes your sorry-ass dog and takes a hunk out of me." He lifted her leash from the nail by the door and wrapped it around his hand. "Took me almost two months of rehabilitation 'cause she tore such a big hole in my ankle and leg. Not to mention what she did to my eye after I fell down."

"You're not welcome here, Clover. You need to turn around and get on home." Andrea squeezed my shoulder. I wished for Jenny. I wished really hard. Where could she be?

"I'm not welcome here? I'm not welcome here? Seems to me that you got yourself backward lady. You two lickers ain't wanted here. And we don't want you putting your wet on our little girl here."

A shadow went by my shoulder. Then another—then another. I wanted to turn to look at where the phantasms might be, but I stood still instead.

He moved forward and clipped the leash to Someday's collar. I was frozen and so was Andrea.

"Leave the dog alone, Clover." Andrea stepped forward and tried to grab the leash.

He grabbed Andrea's arm and spit on the floor. "After I'm done with her, I'm coming back for you." He pulled Andrea down and held her then kissed her on the cheek. "You're going to like it with me better. Guaran-damn-teed." Andrea pulled back but could not seem to free herself from his grip.

Then out of nowhere, three people were in the doorway—Jenny, the social worker and Mr. Wilson, dressed in a suit and tie like he was off to Sunday school.

"Let her go, Clover! Get your stinky hands off of her, you sick, sorry-ass son of a bitch." Jenny charged in toward us.

Clover, as if sensing he was outnumbered, let her go.

"Unclip the dog, Clover," Mr. Wilson said sternly.

Clover sized everyone up and then said, "Mr. Wilson, come on. You don't know what this dog done to me. Look at my leg and my eye."

"Eyes to see, but see not now," Mr. Wilson said, sounding Biblical and all. "Now, I told you once. Unclip the dog and these young ladies won't press charges for trespassing." With that, he folded his arms and it was then that a shiny steel pistol flashed in the light.

Clover undid the leash and dropped it. He headed toward Mr. Wilson, who eyed him the whole way.

"And," Mr. Wilson said, "don't mess with these girls anymore. You think you might be stealthy, but I fought in Vietnam and I know how sick people like you think. Understand?"

Clover kicked the leash on the floor, then turned on a dime and kicked Someday in the side. Someday winced and I went to comfort her. Jenny started to kick him but Andrea stepped in and stopped her. Mr. Wilson never took his eyes off of him.

Then, as quickly as he'd shown up, he was gone.

Mr. Wilson came up to me and said, "You okay?" I nodded. "Your dog okay?" I nodded again. "We've been watching you, you know."

"Who?" I asked.

"Me and Mrs. Wilson." He said it and then nodded to all of us and then him and the clearly stunned social worker left.

And, that was that.

Chapter 12

Within minutes I was whisked away like I had been at the scene of my own crime. A man and a woman both in uniforms put me in the back of what looked like a police car and took me to the jailhouse, as Victor would have called it. I wasn't sure if they had gotten the right criminal. They didn't put any handcuffs on me and the lady who sat beside me talked to me like I was in preschool, asking me what kind of cartoons I liked and did I have any dolls at home. *Who liked dolls?* I thought and didn't say a thing. Incarceration was going to be tough. I'd seen some of the movies Victor watched. The one thing I learned was to keep silent even after they read your rights. They hadn't done that yet, so I was careful. From the glass of the car window, I saw Andrea and Jenny talking to some other police officers. Someday was barking to beat the band and Andrea had to hold her. They were both talking to the social worker and Jenny was jumping up and down like she was a monkey on crack. I giggled but was nervous. Mr. and Mrs. Wilson hung around and pointed at my apartment while the officer took notes.

After three hours of phone calls and ice cream in the Goochland County Jail, the lady officer sat down and talked to me. She wore a blue uniform but didn't have a gun or anything. I wondered what kind of police force this was.

"Piper." She sat down next to me on the bench.

"Are you going to read me my rights?"

She smiled. "Is that what you think you're here for? Do you think you've done something wrong?"

Boy, was that a loaded question.

"Piper, we are in a precarious position here. Do you understand?"

I nodded.

"We can't take you home to your grandfather's apartment because we have some evidence here that he may not be treating you right. Do you know what I mean?"

"No," I said.

"Well, we have some reports from your neighbors and one from your school that looks like your grandfather drinks a whole lot and is never home. Is that true, honey? Does your grandfather drink a lot?"

I looked down and cried. "Yes, ma'am, he does. Is that

why I'm in jail?"

"No, honey. You're not in jail. You are in child protective services. We are here to help you."

"What about Andrea and Jenny? Can I see them?"

"Andrea and Jenny? Are they your neighbors?"

"Yes, ma'am."

"Well, let me see here." She shuffled through some papers, her pencil propped in her hand. She made three side notes. I counted. When I tried to peek, she stopped. "I see. They are your neighbors who made the report to your school. Carver Middle School, right, Piper?"

"Yes, ma'am. That's my school."

"Good."

"What's going to happen now?" I asked.

"Well, right now, we are going to get you something to eat and some toiletries and then I am going to take you to a shelter. Do you know what a shelter is?"

"Like the dog shelter?"

She laughed. "No, not a dog shelter. This is a people shelter for young girls like you. You are going to stay there pending a court hearing to see what to do about where you are best fit to live. Does that make sense?"

"Yes, ma'am."

"You can call me Terri. My name is Terri McCurdy and I am assigned to your case along with your social worker. Do you know her name?"

"The one that came to me and Victor's apartment?"

"Yes. That's the one. Her name is Linda Dougherty. She's the one who called us to come and take a look at all that craziness that was going on in your apartment."

"Okay," I said. "Can my dog come with me?"

"What dog, honey?"

"Someday. My dog. Her name is Someday."

"Where is she honey? Is she with your grandfather?"

"No, she's with Andrea and Jenny. Can she come to the shelter with me?"

"No, honey. I'm sorry, she can't."

My twelve-year-old bones took the last blow my body, mind, spirit and soul could take. I stopped talking right then and there. Clammed right up. I didn't have any rights. They weren't even going to read any to me. But worse, I didn't have my dog. Again. It was the second time I had lost her. I was in another sorry situation. Sorrier than the ones before it felt like.

Terri continued to take notes and put her arm around me—to try and comfort me, I guess. The clock said eight forty-two. It was the third Friday in September. For the next eighteen minutes, I watched the second hand spin around the face of the clock and my mind was empty. Completely empty except for the ticking clock and the scratching of Terri McCurdy's pencil as she sat next to me and filled out forms. I was in full on stare-ation.

At nine p.m., Linda Dougherty showed up with my backpack, more forms, some Goldfish and a Sprite for me. "I think you might like these," she said and handed them over to me. "I noticed plenty of these at your apartment on Stoney Creek. How are we doing, Officer McCurdy? We getting things tidied up so I can get this young lady to her new temporary home?"

"Just about," Terri said. "One thing, though, Linda."

"Yeah."

"I think she's worried about her dog."

"Her dog?"

"Yeah. Her dog."

"I think your neighbors are keeping her till the courts figure out what to do, Piper."

"Can she come with me?" I kept watching the clock and not looking at anyone.

"No, honey. She'll stay with Andrea and Jenny till the judge makes his decision."

"What decision?" I asked and took a swig from my Sprite, then wiped my spit away with the back of my hand.

"About where you're going to live. You'll have a hearing, let me see here, in about a week, right Terri?"

"That's when she's on the schedule."

"Till then, Piper, you'll live in the youth emergency shelter with other girls and a van will take you to Carver. Okay?"

I crunched six Goldfish crackers in my mouth and nodded. I took another long swig of Sprite and wished for a smoke and a sit at my fort. The clock said nine twenty-two exactly.

By nine thirty, I was back in the police car.

The youth emergency shelter was down on Birchcrest Road near the railroad tracks and an old quarry, which wasn't but about fifty yards from the James River. In my mind, I calculated about how far I might be from school and then, of course, school wasn't far from my apartment on Stoney Creek Road. I thought about five miles. That seemed right. Knowing the distance between where I was and where I was supposed to be was a good thing to know in case the fugitive who began to burn inside of me decided on developing a plan.

Grace Baptist Church was across the street from the shelter and the steeple had a bell in it that donged on the hour, every hour. The hardest thing was the numbness, surviving the shadows and the numbness that seemed to anneal to my skin on both the inside and the outside. Stepping outside of my skin would be good, perhaps shed it like a snake and start over. I took stock of my long life. In the span of just a few short years, my life had taken pivots, serious pivots. Jenny had taught me how to pivot. "Plant your foot, Piper"—I could hear her in my mind— "and then spin on it like the earth does on its on axis, except for you're on the ball of your foot." Every time I pivoted, though, somebody went away. My head swirled. Pivot number one—Mom was gone. I missed her voice and her smile and her hugs and her touch, her beautiful, glorious touch that made me feel wanted and loved and alive. Pivot number two—Dad was gone. I wished him back so I could pronounce words right when I read a hard book. Pivot number three—Jack, my playmate, was gone, the crazy soothsayer and warlord of all the red and black ants in the world. I remembered how much he wanted a dog, too. I remembered how much he and I both begged for a dog, and when we finally got one, well, when we got the funky-pawed dog, it was like our whole world was complete. Pivot number four—Someday was separated from me again. If I pivoted again, I would come full circle and lose her, too. I had to stop making mistakes.

This church guilt I carried around sure was heavy.

Now, as I laid in a small bed in a small white room in what smelled like a hospital, I took my pillow and shoved my backpack behind it. I rolled over, shut my eyes and inhaled deeply, searching for the scent of Andrea or Jenny, but mostly for the scent of Someday's fur. The screen window was ajar, and the scent of honeysuckle wafted peculiarly on the wind. I could hear the train thunder in the distance. And in my mind, I prayed. I prayed not this time for my dog, but for me. I prayed for Piper because it was the first time in my life as far as I could remember that I needed help. This time, God, it was too much. *This time, You up there, it's too much. I'm twelve years old, God. Can you give me a break? A little slack in the fishing line, perhaps? Because I don't see the humor in any of this. I'm done. I'm absolutely done. So, if you can take charge and figure this one out for me, I sure would appreciate it. I sure would appreciate it, God.* I said it over and over and over in my head.

One a.m. The train shook my bed. I lifted up in my bed. I felt scared then grabbed my backpack. I pushed my face down on it and dreamed a waking dream. I couldn't get Clover's dumbass face out of my head. Then it was Luke pulling my hair and I was yelling at him to stop. Then I saw Someday in the county pound and she didn't have any legs. Then Victor came along to make the nightmare complete and told me that it was wrong for me to have stayed home the day of the accident. His head was extra big and bulbous and he had worms for stitches on a cut in his face.

Three a.m. The train shook my bed again. I lifted myself up in bed. This time I didn't put my head back down. I'd rather stay awake than have another nightmare.

When I sat there, it was clear the shadows were in the room with me. Looming and floating like dotty molecules. I couldn't make them out. Still, the truth was, they were inside the confines of my cinderblock room.

"Who's there?" I whispered. "Who's there?"

Then I waited. The wind blew the honeysuckle straight up my nose.

"Anyone there? Mom? Are you there?" I waited again.

The hair on my skin stood up, and I could feel the pricklies on my skin. I had chills but was not cold. Chills. The chills were everywhere, like a wave raising their own tide against my tired skin. The hairs on my body stood up like haughty spears as the light wind and its honeysuckle hovered until, like magic, I could smell White Shoulders perfume and my mother's tanned skin.

Then I stopped and hugged myself.

"Hey, Mom!" And the chills got more and more glorious than I had ever felt chills before. My mom wasn't some weird scary gnome. She was an angel and I was feeling her brush right up against my skin like she was touching me for real. She was touching me for real. My mom was in the room with me. The shadow had uncloaked herself. *Thank you, God.*

It was cool to feel her. I had missed her so.

For a very long time, I let my mom sit with me on the side of the bed. It was breathy and palpable. Then when I laid down, she stayed there with me, watching I knew, keeping the glory of her warm chill all over my body as a comfort in my loneliest night. She had named my dog, and let me keep her, and now she brought herself to me and the honeysuckle of Someday's scent on cool air to comfort me. It would imprint me for the rest of my life.

The Giver and Taker Away of all things had brought my mom to me.

Gordon Lightfoot was right. He, God, was reading my mind.

At five a.m., the train rolled by and my shadows were one with me and I understood only one thing. I was not alone.

I stayed in the shelter for several days before I got a sense of the routine. Breakfast was at seven a.m. They rang a bell to wake you up and then everyone went to the community bathroom to wash up and brush teeth. There were girls of all sizes and I made it a point not to talk to anyone. I had less than six years left till I could make it to be a waitress and work at the Curbside and me and Someday would have a place together. I was also, quietly, asking God for a guitar. But after he brought my mom to me as an angel, I tried not to ask too much.

I stayed quiet and shuffled around the girls.

On Tuesday afternoon, the lady in the van dropped me off in front of the shelter and my social worker, Linda

Dougherty, was there. She had some things from my apartment and told me that she'd talked to Andrea and Jenny. Someday and the cats were okay. I asked her when she thought I could go home to them, and she said that when the judge ruled on the case I would know better. She handed me the iPod Jenny had bought me and my skateboard, too. The shelter had a recreation area and I went on my merry way. It would be October soon, and the air was less humid. I hustled from the rec area to my room and grabbed a second shirt and then came back to the double front doors.

Then I saw a good thing.

Jenny had driven up in her postal truck and had a package and some loose envelopes. She barely looked at me and when she walked by she said, "Skate to the edge of the park. Meet me there in three minutes."

I hopped on my board and popped up on the sidewalk and practically cartwheeled on my skateboard all the way to the edge of the rec yard. I sat down and waited.

A few minutes later, Jenny came through the double doors, hustling like she always did when she was delivering mail. She climbed in and zipped all the way to where I was. She threw the truck in park and told me to climb in.

"Thank God you're here. I was wondering how long it was going to take before someone rescued me from that place. Oh, God—" For a second my heart went down to my ankles. Andrea was in the back, sitting in the jumpseat where me and Someday used to ride.

"We're not here to spring you, Piper," Andrea said.

"We're here to have a quick talk and then we have to go before anyone gets suspicious. Okay?" She was real serious and it was scaring me.

"Andrea," I said. "You're scaring me."

Jenny put her hand on my head and said, "Piper, this is a serious situation. Andrea and I are trying to get custody of you through the courts, but we think that us being gay is going to be hurtful to the court letting us have you. Understand?"

Andrea chimed in. "So, Piper, before we continue to do what we think is best for you. We need to ask you what you want. We don't want to do anything until you tell us it's okay. What I mean is this, honey. You need a home. And Jenny and me and a lot of our friends who have watched you these last few months realize that you need help honey. You need a safe place to live and we feel like Victor's is not the safe place for you to be."

"Piper." Jenny leaned down and looked at me eye to eye. "Do you want to come and live with us? Do you want to leave your life with Victor to come and be with us?"

I thought for a minute. "Does it mean that I can be with you all of the time with Someday, too—even the cats?"

"Yes, even the cats," Andrea said.

"Do I have to do math?"

"Piper, you are a numbskull. Of course, you will have to do math."

"Okay."

"Okay what, for Christ's sake," Jenny spouted. "What do you want?" The bell tolled at the church.

"I want what we have now. Can we have it the way it's been all this last summer?"

Andrea sighed. "Honey, we can't hide forever. Jenny and I are here to say that we are willing to risk everything if you think you want to be with us. If you want that—if you want to be with us—then we will try and do everything in our power to get custody of you."

"If I can be with you guys, will I have to pay you something?"

"Not a penny," Jenny said.

"I think I'd like that very much then."

"You know it means that Victor will put up a fuss," Andrea said.

"He's full of piss and vinegar," I said. "But mostly he's just full of Budweiser."

They both laughed to beat the band. I did, too.

"Here, Piper, this letter is special delivery—from us. Read it tonight. Okay?" Jenny brushed the top of my head then kissed it.

They left and I knew I had said the right thing. The church bell tolled forty-four minutes later and I skated inside and tore open the letter.

Dear Piper,

We hope you will understand why we are writing to you. We also hope you will understand why we are here at this time. These past few months have been hard on you and Someday, and Jenny and I have realized that you have been through more than what a normal girl should go through. Girls your age don't endure what you have endured.

We have offered up trying to get custody of you, but you must realize that in Virginia the laws work against people like Jenny and me. We can't get married, for one, and it is extremely difficult, if not impossible, to take a child away from her natural family. It is because we are gay and there are many people out there who don't want us to have equal rights. Jenny and I both believe that this is changing and that the new generation of children, like you, will change this. But right now, it is what it is. We don't have much say in the Virginia courts. You must understand this before the hearing.

We have found out that Victor has hired an attorney from the Flechinstein law firm. We have found out that these people will do anything to win and get their money. Anything, Piper. You may have seen them on TV. But, Piper, they aren't good people. They will stoop to doing just about anything to win a case. They are the most corrupt people in the litigation business.

So, with all that said, Piper, we want you to know that you have a chance to be with us in a different way if it comes down to that. Sometimes taking a different, perhaps more difficult, route is better. So, what we are trying to say is this. Be ready. Be ready to go a different way after the custody hearing. Okay?

We love you, Piper. Both of us have been through a lot from our own past experiences and we are not going to sit back and let anything else happen to you. Understand? Enough is enough. We get it.

Just remember, if you feel something in your heart and believe it to be true, then it is.

All our love,
Andrea and Jenny

P.S. Precious Pink and the kitties say, "Meow." Someday watches through our front window for you to come. She says to not worry and that everything will be all right.

I read it over several times to get the full gist. Then I attempted one of Mrs. Svette's math worksheets. I put my name in the upper right-hand corner, then I fell asleep till the morning sun brought the honeysuckle scent through my window. Courage. Like in *The Wizard of Oz*. I was going to need cup of courage.

As soon as I woke up, I read the letter again. A bucket of courage was more like it. They were right. Enough was enough.

Chapter 13

A few days later, it was the first Thursday in October and we were all lined up in what looked like church pews in the Goochland Juvenile and Domestic Relations Court. The best part so far was that I was missing four worksheets in Mrs. Svette's math class. I was also missing out on reading Edgar Allan Poe "The Raven." We were studying all one hundred and thirty-four lines in our English class and that bird gave me the creeps. All that rapping and tapping on the door and it being dark and midnight. Yuck. Edgar Poe did, too. All that black and how he could marry his thirteen-year-old first cousin grossed me out. It reminded me of something Clover might do. In my mind I could see him yelling at his child bride, "Hey, get me another beer." Then he would say, "Come sit on my lap and open it for me." *Quish*. Why I had that dumbass image in my brain, I did not know. I did not want to think about Edgar Poe or Clover. I pulled at my pressed shirt that the lady at the shelter let me wear and wiped my hands on my jeans. I leaned over and tied my brother's Dekline skating shoes I had on and then fingered the two things I had in my right front pocket— the letter that Andrea and Jenny had written to me that I had read twenty-eight times since I had seen them a few days earlier and some honeysuckle I had pulled off of the bush outside of my window at the shelter.

Officer Terri McCurdy, who had picked me up from school, sat on one side of me looking at the front of the room and every now and again got up and went to the side and talked with another officer. Linda Dougherty flanked me on the other side and shuffled through papers and asked me every nine and a half seconds if I was comfortable. I just kept nodding my head and putting my hand in my front pocket where I rolled the honeysuckle in between my forefinger and my thumb. We were in the second pew back from the front.

The double doors opened in the back and everyone turned to look.

It was Victor. Unbelievable. He wore a blue suit, had shaved his salt-and-pepper scraggly beard off and his hair was neatly trimmed. I remembered in the letter how Jenny and Andrea had said that the law firm had a reputation for being the nastiest, crookedest, cheapest rogues in the litigation business. Or something like that. I couldn't remember. *Nervous.* My hands got sweaty. I did not understand the word *litigation* but knew from the tone of the letter that the lawyer he'd hired might be trouble. The attorney lady wore a tight business suit and had big red strawberry-blonde hair and wore more makeup than Tammy Faye Baker. Her arm was cradled in his arm and they practically crawled to the left pew. I tried to wave but neither one of them looked at me. If she was like this Poe guy, then I was in trouble. I rubbed my sweaty hands on my legs and looked at Linda Dougherty.

"It's okay," she said.

I glanced at Terri McCurdy as she eyed my grandfather and spoke in whispers to her uniformed friend.

Then, practically a minute later, Andrea and Jenny came through the double doors. I looked back again and caught Jenny's eye immediately. She winked at me and I waved. Andrea was talking to some guy who was with her so I did not try to distract her by waving. I half expected Someday to walk right in behind them. When I had this thought, a warm chill made the hair on the back of my neck raise up. I smiled. *Good girl.*

Both Andrea and Jenny stopped halfway up the aisle to talk to Lucy and Alma and Brock. I was glad they were there as an unexpected surprise. I entertained the thought to wave at them, too. But then, suddenly, I was turned around by Ms. Dougherty, who told me to stand up. I wasn't sure what for and watched Andrea and Jenny and the young man, their lawyer, slide into the chairs at the table in the front of the courtroom.

As I stood, I started to count. There were sixteen

people in the room.

There was a lady with thick round glasses up at the front and she was typing on a typewriter. She kept looking at some notes and then typing. Terri McCurdy and five uniformed officers—some in blue, some in brown—stood against the wall next to the bench where the judge sat. I'd seen Judge Judy with Victor, so the setup looked a little familiar. There were some other people I did not recognize who must have been there for other reasons. It was not clear. I rubbed the honeysuckle again and looked up at the ceiling of the courtroom.

A microphone stand was in the middle between the two tables of the people who were going for my life. Victor and his lawyer sat on the left side. Space. Aisle. Jenny and Andrea and their lawyer on the other.

We were all up on our feet because the bailiff had said the "all rise" part for Judge Harry Stonack to enter the room. He took his sweet time as I was beginning to count the paneling on the wall.

Then he came. White-haired, belly scratching—Stronack. He looked heavy and rotund and moved like he was a backward bovine.

"You may be seated," the bailiff said, and we sat. His balding head had a row of hair in the middle that was sticking up slightly. Every now and again, he reached up and slicked it back. He rifled through some papers—evidently he wasn't slow at that—and then asked for the state's evidence.

I was sort of shocked to see Terri McCurdy walk to the front and address the judge at the microphone.

"In case number sixty-seven ninety-three dash four, we have a juvenile, a Piper Leigh Cliff, who has been in the custody of her paternal grandfather since the deaths of her mother, father and brother over two years ago. She resides at twelve nineteen Stoney Creek Drive in the Walton apartment complex in Goochland County. She attends Carver Middle School where she is a seventh-grader who excels in reading. Her teachers describe her as a quiet teenager who has a few friends. A Ms. Andrea Winter and Ms. Jenny Black say she's friendly with them and the neighborhood children. They are her neighbors who live three doors down and were the ones who first alerted the school. The school assigned their psychologist, who interviewed Piper Leigh Cliff. After these interviews, the psychologist and the school then contacted child protective services to investigate in the case of Piper Leigh Cliff and Victor Cliff and the alleged misconduct of neglect and possible child abuse."

Stronack cleared his gruffy throat and spoke. "Thank you, Ms. McCurdy." He shifted in his chair and looked at us. "As most of you know, in child custody cases, we must hear from both sides in the case. We have a Mr. Victor Cliff. Please identify yourself, Mr. Cliff."

Victor stood up and raised his hand. He sat down quickly and leaned into his attorney, who put her hand on his back.

"Thank you, Mr. Cliff. And we have two women, a Ms. Black and Ms. Winter who are neighbors of the juvenile. Please identify yourselves."

Jenny and Andrea stood up and raised their hands.

Jenny had dropped the postal uniform and donned a black pantsuit with a white shirt over her collar and shiny black shoes. Andrea wore a bright pink dress with pearls. They were handsome, I thought.

"Thank you."

There were more preliminary this-and-thats. My mind began to wander around the courtroom and I thought of Someday for some weird reason: the shriveled paw, her time in captivity, how she was nestled in with Precious Pink and the kittens. I was skipping through all parts of my brain. I landed in math class, thought of my skateboard, and then it all went away when I saw Victor approach the microphone.

"Uh, ahem." He cleared his throat. "Your Honor, my name is Victor Cliff and I'm Piper's grandfather." His hands shook while he buttoned his coat. "I believe that there has been a big mistake in all of this and I wanted to get a few things straight. Now, I know I ain't been the best of grandfathers and on occasion took to drinkin'. But you see, Your Honor, just two years ago I lost my son and his wife and my only grandson. It's been hard and I think I been a little off. Off kilter somehow. I don't know, but Piper and I here have made a decent home." He turned and looked at me and waved. On instinct, I waved back. "See"—he paused and averted his gaze—"she's the only thing I have left. I ain't got no next a kin and my wife's gone. She's got an aunt who don't want nothing to do with her. So, it's been me and her. And now—" He buckled. "And now, ya'll gone and took her away." He teared up and glared at Andrea and Jenny. "These two women called the school and then the social worker came and everything's been a mess since. I have a good pension and I just recently joined Alcoholics Anonymous. I even have a letter here from my sponsor. So, I don't know. I need another chance, Your Honor. I'm trying to clean my act up and want very much to keep my granddaughter. I hope that if you have children of your own, you'll understand. She's all I got. Everything. She's everything to me. Thank you."

He blubbered his snot into a tissue and I felt sorry for him. My grandfather was a mess. He drank all day and all night and peed all over himself. If alcoholics were anonymous, he had just announced his anonymity to the whole world and that lady typed it all down.

The judge put his hand up. "Wait, Mr. Cliff. Hand that letter to the court officer." He handed it over and the court officer handed it up to Judge Stronack. "Thank you, Mr. Cliff. I'll take a look at this. When's the last time you had a drink?"

Victor got up. "September twenty-sixth, Your Honor." He sat down. I counted the number of days he'd been on the wagon. Then out of nowhere, I felt a warm chill.

Victor's lawyer got up and said a few things about how this was an open-and-shut case and that the "child should be remanded back to her grandfather immediately. The family has been through enough in the last few years and clearly Mr. Cliff is on the right path to recovery. Case closed." She gave the court reporter some documents and sat next to Victor.

Stronack waited for the court typist to catch up. "Now,

let's hear from you, uh, Mr.—"

"Holden, Your Honor, Clay Holden." He popped up like a prairie dog next to Andrea and Jenny and walked to the microphone. "Your Honor, we have a strong case here on behalf of Piper Cliff. If I may, let me just read to you from some notes and the evidence that the social worker has given me."

The judge nodded his head and pushed his glasses up. I turned around and gave a gentle wave to Alma and Lucy. They waved back.

"Your Honor, we have quite a problem here—"

"Wait, young man, I'll decide if there is a problem or not." The judge scooted his chair forward.

"Well, let me just tell you the evidence. On the first three visits from the social worker, a Ms. Linda Dougherty, she noted the following: the residence at twelve nineteen Stoney Creek Drive was clean, but there was minimal food and drink in the refrigerator. There were few items that a child of Piper's age might have in her room. In other words, there were sheets and a blanket on her bed and that was it. No radio, no CDs; barely any clothes in her closet. The residence smelled of smoke. There were four cartons of cigarettes on the kitchen table and in the dining room; there were four shotguns locked in a cabinet along with six or seven hunting and fishing knives lying on the table. On the fourth and unannounced visit . . ."

He told it all, from Victor lying on the couch in his own urine, to him never being home, to him leaving me at church by myself, to him leaving me at home for hours sometimes nights all by myself while he drank and fished and used the money from the accident to fuel his drinking habits, to the no food, to the unending alcohol, to the no counseling for me for my own losses, to his best friend Clover trying to steal my dog and hurt it on the last visit by the social worker. He told the judge how Andrea and Jenny and me had met in June and how since the Fourth of July, these two nice women had been taking care of not only me and my needs as an adolescent but also my dog, Someday.

"Who?" the judge asked.

"Someday. Uh. Your Honor, the dog's name is Someday."

"I've never heard of a dog named a name like that. What in the world?" he mumbled. "Continue, Mr. Holden."

When Mr. Holden said the word *Someday*, Victor got torqued up like a pimple ready to pop. The lights in the courtroom flickered and Victor stood up and blurted it out. "That dog, Your Honor, should have been put to sleep. That crazy lame dog bit my close friend Clover and nearly put his eye out and tore a hole through his calf—"

"Hold on, Mr. Cliff. You'll have another turn." The judge motioned for him to sit.

"That dog should have been put down, she's a danger to my friend and my granddaughter—"

"Mr. Cliff, sit down." The judge was stern.

Between my forefinger and my thumb, I rubbed the honeysuckle to pieces in my pocket. Victor had said it. I was stunned. Unbelievable. The worst thing he could have said. *Put Someday down.* He had wanted my dog dead 'cause she'd taken a hunk out of slimy Clover. He had done it before and now he wanted to do it again.

I'd had it. I'd had it and I'd done a lot of thinking. Thinking and praying—praying and thinking. I came full damn circle, right then and there. Full circle.

It was a turning point in my young life that even now I do not regret. A pivotal point. I'd remembered Vera talking about time standing still at Andrea and Jenny's party before she took off to Canada. My brain boiled. My fists clenched. I thought about the kittens but I did not care. Victor had crossed the line and I had lost everything—my mom, my dad, my brother—and now I believed in my soul of souls that I was on the verge of losing Someday again. I would not—I could not stand for it. He had said those words: *put down*. I hadn't seen my dog in nearly a week.

I prayed to my mother to give me a bucket of courage. Now. Right now.

The lights dimmed in the courtroom.

I put both hands in the air and I stood up. I think I scared my social worker and half knocked her into the aisle.

"V-i-c-t-o-r-r-r-r-r-r-r-r-r-r!" I yelled in the courtroom. "V-i-c-t-o-r-r-r-r-r-r-r-r-r-r!" I yelled again. The social worker told me to sit down. She pulled on me and I told her to get her hands off of me. I leapt like a cat over her and into the aisle of the courtroom. I was out of my mind. I yelled and burbled like a Pentecostal on fire at anything and everything in front of me.

"Young lady!" Judge Stronack scolded. "Young lady—"

Victor turned and glared at me with his gin-blossomed face.

I screamed at him and everyone. "You can't take her and me away. You son of a bitch. You can't take my dog away. You say I'm the only one you have. Well, she's the only one I have. You hear me? Victor! Victor! Victor! I don't care how many kittens die. Let the kittens die. Let them die. Don't you take my dog away. Don't you take my dog away. She needs me, Victor! Leave her alone. You hear me? Leave her alone. Stop it. Stop it all. You leave my good girl alone. Do you hear me?"

Terri McCurdy grabbed me on one side and the social worker grabbed me on the other side.

I yelled for Jenny. "Jenny! Jenny! Help me. Don't let them take my dog away." I started sobbing.

Jenny moved into the aisle and the judge slammed his gavel down sixteen billion times but I wasn't counting.

"You took them to heaven, Victor. Tell the truth. You took them to heaven. Mom and Dad and Jack. You drove the truck that night. You were driving the truck that night, Victor. I remember now. The beer can next to the truck and you ran that red light and that car slammed right into my mother's side of the car. It was you who drove the truck that night and killed everybody. Admit it. Admit it. Admit it. All you got was twenty-four damn stitches in your lame-ass head. I heard you say it when you were drunk, Victor. You drove my parents and my brother to heaven. Now, don't you take my dog away, again. I know about the first time, Victor. I know about how you lied about trying to find her in the pound. You never went looking for her. You're the one that killed my family then tried to kill my dog."

"What are you talking about, Piper?" Victor moved into the aisle next to Jenny. They were side by side coming toward me. The lights flickered again.

"I saw you. I saw you get into the truck and take them away."

"Good grief, Piper. What are you thinkin'? You know damn well I wasn't there."

Lucy and Alma came up the aisle. I struggled against Linda Dougherty and Terri McCurdy.

Lucy darted around. "Here, let go. I've got her." For some reason they both let go.

"I want to be with Jenny and Andrea," I said to Lucy. "Why can't I just go home with them?" I yelled and asked all at once. "I promise to be good. I promise I won't smoke or anything."

"Smoke?" Lucy said. "You been smoking?"

I hurled my vitriolic spit at Victor. "You wrecked the truck, Victor. Admit it!"

Victor and I were at an impasse, a Mexican standoff. He looked at his lawyer, then the judge, and then back at me. Then, like he was his own biggest loser, he just suddenly gave up and said the worst thing anyone could or would ever say to me. "It should have been you, Piper. It should have been you who cut your hand and had to go to the hospital. It should have been you instead of your brother. You should have been in that truck instead of back at home with that three-legged lump of fur you call a dog."

Then the lights went out. Completely. Everyone got exasperated for a minute, but as our eyes adjusted, I could make out the shape of the pews and the outline of the courtroom. Lucy dropped my hand.

The tumult that followed remained nebulous in my mind's eye. People shuffled. The judge called for the courtroom to come to order but no one was paying any attention to anyone. It was chaotic.

As Lucy let me go, a shadow of someone grabbed my shoulder and pulled me through the double doors. I could not see who it was because I was crying like a baby. Everything hurt. As I exited, I overheard Lucy barking at Jenny and Andrea to get out.

"There's no use," Lucy said. "This judge's nickname is Strong Ass and he'd never let any gay girls get custody over their own vaginas much less a young girl."

Jenny and Andrea met me out back. How I got there, I could not remember. But all they said was, "Let's hurry. We don't have much time."

"I can hardly breathe," I said.

Jenny said, "Tough, you can breathe later. Right now we need to run."

So, we did.

Chapter 14

We only had a few hours to pack. I learned later that Lucy and Alma stayed back at the courthouse and somehow convinced Victor to go with them to the Curbside. He didn't know who they were, he'd told them, but Lucy explained that she had been a custody lawyer for quite a while and that Alma was her assistant. Apparently, they bought him eight beers and a shot of tequila. After a couple of hours, they left him in the booth and hustled to Brock Goldberg's house and doctored up some papers with a high-tech printer and some notarized stamps. Brock said he could manage anything with a digital camera and some solid stock paper. Four phone calls were made to Banff, Canada, where Vera Curran resided. On the fourth, Vera said it was a no-damn-brainer and she would be fine with the mission. It was a mission I had never floated around nor dreamed about. But, I think my mom and dad and Jack floated over Goochland County till Andrea and Jenny and me and Someday and Precious Pink and the kittens could get into the Dodge pickup truck and hustle out of town.

Prior to leaving, Someday followed me around Andrea and Jenny's apartment while they gathered some things. Andrea wrote a long note to Lucy, Alma and Brock telling them to ship a few items and sell the rest. The kittens were two and a half weeks old and Pink hollered a bit when they all went into the big crate, but Someday licked her and the kittens. That seemed to shut her up for a while.

I asked them what we were doing. Jenny said that we were taking a long trip to see Vera. I said, "Cool." I liked her.

"Well, I hope you do," Andrea told me, "because we were going away for a very long time."

We loaded up the pickup truck and as we gathered up our last few items, I clipped the leash onto Someday.

Andrea opened the side cab door and I helped Someday up. She would be three in November, I thought. I kissed her in between her eyes. Jenny put the crate in the camper. An image suddenly flickered on my shoulder, and then like manna from heaven, Mrs. Wilson appeared at the end of the curb. She had on a blue flowered housecoat and was cradling something in her hand. I couldn't make out what it was till she got closer.

"Piper?" she said. It was the first time she'd ever addressed me. She sounded coy and crackly like her windpipes were rusty with age.

"Yes, ma'am," I said.

Jenny and Andrea looked at each other and stopped what they were doing.

Mrs. Wilson was in front of me. "Piper," she said again, "I've been wanting to give this to you." She held out the Celtic Cross I'd thrown in the yard in the summertime when Someday had gone missing. "Remember when you threw this out the window last summer?"

"Yes, ma'am."

"Well, I thought it might be important, so I went and got it and saved it for you. It's a pretty cross. Is it yours?"

"No, ma'am. It was my mom's."

"Oh, I see. She wore this. Well, I bet it was one of her favorites. My mother gave me a pendant when I was a young woman. See?" She pulled it out from under her housecoat. A shimmery white gold pendant with an inscription on it that was too worn for me to make out.

"It's pretty," I said.

"Your mama is dead, I know. I remember her from church. She was a good woman. Boy, did she love you. I know she's in heaven right now"—she looked up to the sky—"watching over you. You wear this for her. It's yours now. You've earned it, Piper. Understand?"

"Yes, ma'am."

Mrs. Wilson's shaky hands went around my neck and she clipped it to me. She hugged me and I hugged her back. "Now," she said, wiping my forehead, "when you come home, come see Mr. Wilson and me, hear?"

"Yes, ma'am. I promise." I climbed into the truck with my hand on the cross.

On the first leg of the trip, we passed the shelter where Someday had lived for three days. Shaneefa was getting in her car. Andrea quickly pulled over and asked if we could buy a leash from her for Someday and get a tag. We would need one for the dog to cross the border. I fingered the cross on my neck. Shaneefa spied all of us and tagged us for runaways right away. She grinned her gold-toothed smile.

She opened the door to the pound, clearly proud that they had finally given her keys. She made a tag for Someday and printed out vaccination and rabies certificates.

Andrea gave her sixty dollars. And then, Shaneefa asked her what I had been wanting to ask the both of them. She came to the side of the truck and Jenny rolled the window down. Andrea got in the driver's seat.

"Why you doin' all this? Hey, funky-pawed dog!" She scratched Someday behind her ear.

"My parents abandoned me when I was seventeen years old," Andrea said. "I promised myself then that I'd never witness that kind of cruelty again. So, we're taking this one away from it—all of it."

"What dey do dat fo?" Shaneefa said.

"My parents?" Andrea said. "My parents left me because—"

"Because we're big bad gay people," Jenny interjected.

"Das it? Cuz ya'll two le'bians? Shoo. Girl. I tell you. I been wif bofe. And if you ax me, doin' it wif a gih ain't no different from a guy. 'Quipment lil off. But, dat's it. Shoo. Kissin' is kissin'. Lovin' is lovin'. You evah need somfin, you call me, hear? If you yell's my name loud enough, I hear."

The first Amber Alert went off for me—I found out later—over twenty-four hours after we'd left Goochland, then Richmond, then Virginia, then America. We sailed into Canada free—no problem at all.

As we drove, I held the fur of my funky-pawed dog, put my head on the backseat and let the drumming of the wheels take me inside to my thoughts, my own wheels of memory and motion.

Earlier that year, I had floated in my apartment pool after I had wrecked my skateboard. Two girls had run into me and nearly killed me. One named Jenny, who cussed like a sailor and could arc a ball into a hoop from over thirty feet away, had poured cool water over my bruised head. I did not know that later the memory would make me feel like I had been newly baptized. The other, Andrea, who helped rescue my dog from the shelter, had read my Tarot cards: the four of Cups, the Tower, the Empress, and the last card I'd pulled on that Fourth of July was the World card. The World in the major arcana, Andrea had told me, meant fulfillment. And, now, they were taking me to a place where I could be safe and read and excel in math.

I had dreamed that when I was eighteen I would leave Victor and work at the Curbside Café and that Someday and I would live in an apartment complex nearby.

It would never happen.

Six years later, I came back to Virginia because my grandfather lay dying. Six years later, I had a pickup truck, my third iPod, seven pairs of jeans, four denim shirts, a brown Fender guitar and my dog, Someday. Six years later, Someday and me traveled the four thousand miles from Banff, Canada, back to Goochland, Virginia. Her head and ears floated in the wind through half of Canada and most of the United States. Six years later I wore my mother's cross, still. Six years later Alma would tell me in a conversation on the phone that I had made a date with the best monosyllabic word of them all: *free.* In Canada, we were free.

I never tied Someday to a tree again. I kept her water bowl full, got her annual shots and walked her on the streets of my new small town with my "parents," Jenny Black-Winter and Andrea Black-Winter. My parents who gave up everything they had to take a chance on a little girl like me. Until them, I didn't even know I existed. I accepted and loved all cats. I relearned cause and effect. I fell in love with my first girl on a basketball court at Banff High School. When I wrapped my arms around her and kissed her in a dimly lit gym one dark December night, my knees melted and I thought my tongue would catch fire.

Vera Curran taught me everything in her curious ways. I read one hundred and fifty of the greatest books of all time, including *To Kill a Mockingbird*. She said that it was the most pivotal book of the twentieth century. I agreed. It had worked for me, too—in more ways than one. Vera made me study grammar and literature—no math. "Math sucks," she'd say. We had long talks about anything and everything and, ironically, I learned what an indefinite pronoun was. I learned, too, that my dog was deaf in one ear—trauma, the vet told me, no doubt from a bad kick in the head on one hot, sticky Fourth of July. She wasn't "indeafinite"—instead she was definite . . . definitely in me, and I, I was in her.

For whatever reason, God had taken Mom, Dad and my brother to heaven long before I'd ever wanted Him to. He'd left me with Someday—the funky-pawed dog who had found me by the James River one day by a rickety pier where my mom had taught me to skitter rocks. The dog who'd bit Crazy Clover and saved me from his creepy grip. The dog who had followed me everywhere, from my dirty fort in the woods to the swimming pool to four hundred postal stops while Jenny and I sang along to "Fool in the Rain." The dog who'd travel four thousand miles to a place where Andrea and Jenny and Vera and I could live safely because things in Canada were cold and free. The dog who'd saved my life in more ways than I could imagine. She was my good girl.

Nobody, not even God, would ever take my Someday away.

I was counting—this time—on my heart for that.

Publications from Spinsters Ink

P.O. Box 242
Midway, Florida 32343
Phone: 800-301-6860
www.spinstersink.com

MERMAID by Michelene Esposito. When May unearths a box in her missing sister's closet she is taken on a journey through her mother's past that leads her not only to Kate but to the choices and compromises, emptiness and fullness, the beauty and jagged pain of love that all women must face. ISBN 978-1-883523-85-5 $14.95

ASSISTED LIVING by Sheila Ortiz Taylor. Violet March, an eighty-two-year-old resident of Casa de los Sueños, finally has the opportunity to put years of mystery reading to practical use. One by one her comrades, the Bingos, are dying. Is this natural attrition, or is there a plot afoot? ISBN 978-1-883523-84-2 $14.95

NIGHT DIVING by Michelene Esposito. *Night Diving* is both a young woman's coming-out story and a 30-something coming-of-age journey that proves you can go home again.
ISBN 978-1-883523-52-7 $14.95

FURTHEST FROM THE GATE by Ann Roberts. *Furthest from the Gate* is a humorous chronicle of a woman's coming of age, her complicated relationship with her mother and the responsibilities to family that last a lifetime. ISBN 978-1-883523-81-7 $14.95

EYES OF GRAY by Dani O'Connor. Grayson Thomas was the typical college senior with typical friends, a typical job and typical insecurities about her future. One Sunday morning, Gray's life became a little less typical, she saw a man clad in black, and started doubting her own sanity. ISBN 978-1-883523-82-4 $14.95

ORDINARY FURIES by Linda Morgenstein. Tired of hiding, exhausted by her grief after her husband's death, Alexis Pope plunges into the refreshingly frantic world of restaurant resort cooking and dining in the funky chic town of Guerneville, California. ISBN 978-1-883523-83-1 $14.95

A POEM FOR WHAT'S HER NAME by Dani O'Connor. Professor Dani O'Connor had pretty much resigned herself to the fact that there was no such thing as a complete woman. Then out of nowhere, along comes a woman who blows Dani's theory right out of the water. ISBN 1-883523-78-8 $14.95

WOMEN'S STUDIES by Julia Watts. With humor and heart, *Women's Studies* follows one school year in the lives of three young women and shows that in college, one's extracurricular activities are often much more educational than what goes on in the classroom. ISBN 1-883523-75-3 $14.95

THE SECRET KEEPING by Francine Saint Marie. *The Secret Keeping* is a high-stakes, girl-gets-girl romance, where the moral of the story is that money can buy you love if it's invested wisely. ISBN 1-883523-77-X $14.95

DISORDERLY ATTACHMENTS by Jennifer L. Jordan. The fifth Kristin Ashe Mystery. Kris investigates whether a mansion someone wants to convert into condos is haunted. ISBN 1-883523-74-5 $14.95

VERA'S STILL POINT by Ruth Perkinson. Vera is reminded of exactly what it is that she has been missing in life. ISBN 1-883523-73-7 $14.95

Visit

Spinsters Ink

at

SpinstersInk.com

or call our toll-free number

1-800-301-6860